POISON PASS

Heaven by day and hell by night, Revelation Pass is an enigma. Ruled by a mercurial preacher and his hardcases, the town endures a monthly lottery that sacrifices young women to a mysterious fate. When former manhunter Jim Hannigan is hired to find a runaway daughter he expects a quick mission with minimum risk – until he discovers the girl swinging from a cottonwood at the town's entrance. Now, buried secrets and hidden motives threaten to embroil Hannigan in the most deadly case of his career.

D0573986

POISON PASS

POISON PASS

by

Lance Howard

Dales Large Print Books
Long Preston, North Yorkshire,
BD23 4ND, England.

British Library Cataloguing in Publication Data.

Howard, Lance
    Poison pass.

    A catalogue record of this book is
    available from the British Library

    ISBN   978-1-84262-618-4 pbk

First published in Great Britain 2006 by Robert Hale Limited

Copyright © Howard Hopkins 2006

Cover illustration © Gordon Crabb by arrangement with
Alison Eldred

The right of Howard Hopkins to be identified as the author of
this work has been asserted by him in accordance with the
Copyright, Designs and Patents Act, 1988

Published in Large Print 2008 by arrangement with
Robert Hale Ltd.

Dales Large Print is an imprint of Library Magna Books Ltd.

Printed and bound in Great Britain by
T.J. (International) Ltd., Cornwall, PL28 8RW

For Tannenbaum

CHAPTER ONE

'You know we've got no choice in the matter, Quimby.' Bertrim Hanely cleared his throat, his bloodshot eyes locking on the man sitting across the table. He didn't like the situation any better than Quimby, but the lottery had to be held and that was that. All the argument in the West, all the guilt sweating from every pore, wouldn't change the task ahead of them this night – the second night running the Council of Three had been summoned to perform its unenviable duty.

'Jesus, Hanely, it ain't human what he asks us to do.' Jacob Quimby squirmed in his chair, eyelids fluttering like the wings of a dying moth. His thick eyebrows, graying, as were his mutton-chop side-whiskers, nearly met in the middle. He bit at his lower lip to keep it from trembling. He stiffened suddenly, chin jutting, a spark of resolve overriding the fear and disgust in his soul. The shopkeeper hammered a fist against the table. The kerosene lantern's flame danced, its buttery light jittering across the walls of the small room above the general store. Shadows swayed across their faces and cavorted over the scuffed floorboards. A battered Stetson placed in the middle of the table jumped, wobbled to a standstill.

'I'm sick and tired of him whipping us like helpless curs!' Quimby's voice came a hair steadier. 'If we ganged up on him–'

'He'd kill us all. Christ, Quimby, we go through this argument every damn time we meet. Doesn't do us a lick of good. No good at all.' The words came from the third man at the table, sitting at the end, facing the door opposite. John Hallet dragged the back of his thin hand across his brow and pinched his lips closed. A slight man with mousy hair and papery skin, Hallet was the least honorable of the three, in Bertrim Hanely's estimation – if, indeed, any of them deserved that label after the acts they'd been driven to commit. Hallet was the one most likely to go shooting off his mouth to that devil in a holy man's collar. The town couldn't afford that; *they* couldn't afford that. Hanely had little taste for what he was doing but he had a big taste for life, one he wanted to go on sampling.

The room remained quiet for dragging

moments. The acrid odor of sweat assailed Hanely's nostrils ... no, not sweat: fear. The stench of fear. The room was hot as the Devil's furnace and each man perspired profusely, but summer heat had little to do with what soured the air. For no matter how much they resented their duty, no matter how much it repulsed them; no matter how detestable they'd become as men, as human beings, it did not compare to the fear that hovered around them because of one man and his iron grip over this town.

Quimby stared at the hat in the center of the table, some of his backbone withering. 'It's worse this time.'

'It's worse every time.' Bertrim Hanely twisted at the end of his handlebar mustache. 'It won't get any easier. Ever. Why put ourselves through hell every lottery?'

Quimby shook his head. Sweat trickled down his face and dripped onto his brocade vest. He suddenly looked ten years older than his forty seasons on this earth. 'He's gone plumb loco, Hanely.'

'His lack of sanity was never in question.' Hallet shifted in his chair, brow knitting. 'No sane man would force us to hold this lottery every month.'

'His men are everywhere.' A defeated look

11

crossed Hanely's rough features. Lantern-flame shimmered through the pomade in his dark hair, parted in the middle. 'Some we know about, like Bartlett. Others are in place among the townsfolk; we don't know whom to trust.' Hanely cast a glance at Hallet, which the mousy man ignored.

Quimby frowned. 'Don't matter. How many can there be?'

'Enough to kill each and everyone of us twice over!' Hallet's tone darkened. 'You think I wouldn't have done something about it by now in my newspaper if I thought there wasn't a score of his men just waiting on his order to run this town to hell?'

Quimby's eyes narrowed. 'Would you, Hallet? Would you really?'

'Now see here–' Hallet's teeth slid together and Quimby braced himself, but Hanely stepped in before they came to blows.

'Christ, isn't this hard enough without you two constantly at each other's throats?' His voice came sharp, raised, but with an edge of fear. 'Let's just get on with it. Bill's crazy as they come. We all know that. It changes nothing.'

'Two nights in a row, Hanely...' Quimby's gaze shifted to the huskier man. 'And he left that poor girl's body right where anyone ridin' in will see it, for chrissakes. He's never done that before.'

Hanely sighed. 'I know, I know. He's gotten worse, but it was our fault for giving him that girl. She wasn't pure. We took the easy way out 'cause she wasn't one of our own. We can't always be sure 'bout the outsiders.'

'She was still a human being.' Quimby's face tightened into annoyed lines. 'She don't deserve to be hanging there for the buzzards. If some lawdog passes through we'll end up hanging along next to her.'

Hanely's lips pressed together. Hallet peered at some invisible spot on the table.

Quimby let out a disgusted sound. 'We aren't men anymore. He's turned us into sheep and in the end we'll be led to slaughter whether we do his bidding or not. His kind doesn't give a damn about honor or life.'

'He's made this town, Quimby.' Hallet's voice came shaky. 'It's a haven during the day.'

Quimby's eyes darkened as they focused on Hallet. 'I best didn't hear you right, John. I swear you were just defending the man.'

Hallet's face flushed with guilt. 'Hell, you know I wasn't, Quimby. I'm just saying ... things could be worse.'

'Worse than sending one of our girls to

some unknown fate at that bastard's hands?'

'Only thing that keeps this town from being more than a pile of smoldering ash.' Hallet's voice carried a defiant note.

Quimby stared at him a moment. 'You don't have a daughter, do you, Hallet? No children. Fact, I hear tell you haven't touched that wife of yours in quite a spell–'

'Now see here, you sonofa–' Hallet came half out of his seat.

Quimby rose to meet him, muscles tensing across his face and neck. 'No, *you* see here, you little turncoat. That gal hanging out there was someone's daughter. It's downright loathsome what he did to her. I have half a mind to cut her down and give her a decent burial.'

'But you won't, Quimby,' Bertrim Hanely said, eyes hard. 'You won't because you know what he'd do and how many people will die.'

Quimby's chin knotted, trembled, but after a moment he lowered himself back into the seat. 'It ain't right ... it just ain't right.'

'Let's get on with it.' Hallet settled back into his chair. 'We're just wasting time and if he comes lookin' for us that gal will have company. The law won't find her. The buzzards will pick her bones clean 'fore that ever happens.'

Quimby shuddered. Lines of sweat ran down his face.

All three stared at the Stetson in the center of the table. None seemed eager to reach for it.

'It's your turn, Quimby,' Hallet said, with almost a note of glee in his voice. Hanely assumed it was from nerves, but a brittle voice deep in his mind raised a suspicion that the mousy newspaperman actually derived some sort of perverse pleasure from their monthly ritual.

Quimby's eyes darted. For long seconds he refused to look back to the hat. With a deep breath he suddenly plunged a hand into the Stetson, snatching out a slip of paper from the many piled within.

He sat still another moment, sliding his jaw back and forth, keeping the paper folded, eyes reflecting his fear of opening it and peering at the name scribbled across the yellowed slip.

They'd done it over twenty times, now, and it never got easier, Hanely reckoned. Quimby was the softest of them, the most moral, the man most burdened by guilt. He could hardly fault him for that, but it only made it worse on all concerned.

'Open it, Quimby,' Hallet said. 'We don't

want Bill showin' up here. It's best to just get it done quick. Then life goes back to normal with tomorrow's sunrise.'

Quimby peered at the mousy newspaper-man and scoffed. 'Normal?' His tone carried a bitter note, but his eyes shifted to the folded paper in his hand. Drawing a sharp breath and holding it, he opened the slip.

His hand started to quake, as his eyes focused on the name written on the paper. Shaking his head, his lips parted, mouthing a silent 'No'. The paper dropped from his fingers.

'Who is it, Quimby?' Hallet's eyes betrayed a peculiar eagerness.

Hanely reached across the table and took the slip, scanning the name. Something in his belly dropped and he folded the paper back over. 'I'm sorry, Quimby...' His voice trickled out, laced with sympathy.

Quimby looked up, tears shimmering in his eyes, lantern-light reflected within, glittering like the flame of original sin. 'No, please, Bertrim, not her. Please.'

Hanely's own hands began to shake. 'I'm sorry, Quimby. You know the rules. You knew it would happen sooner or later.'

'I ... I'd hoped she'd marry by that time ... I'd hoped...'

'I know...' Hanely lifted from his seat, reached across the table and put his hand over Quimby's. 'Be strong, Jacob. Be strong. Your sacrifice will save the lives of many others.'

Quimby's eyes begged Hanely. A tear slipped down his cheek. 'Please, Bertrim. She's my daughter.'

'We got no choice... we got no choice.' Hanely pulled his hand from Quimby's, something twisting deep in his belly. 'Where is she?'

Quimby went silent. His lips trembled and his entire body shook. For a moment Hanely wasn't entirely certain that Quimby wasn't just going to pitch sideways out of his chair in a dead faint. Christ, how would he have felt himself had it been his own daughter? He couldn't even imagine Quimby's pain.

'She's working late at the paper,' Hallet said, standing.

'Why you goddamned—' Quimby shot from his chair, hurling himself at Hallet, who moved as if he had expected the larger man to attack. Quimby stumbled into the table, collapsed against it, bracing both hands against the edge to keep himself from falling.

The color washed from Hallet's face. 'Christ, get hold of yourself, Quimby. You know if Bill sees you this way he'll kill us all. I'm sorry for your loss, but we all gotta live in this town. Ain't no escape. No escape at all.'

Quimby glared at the newspaperman. Hanely wasn't sure Quimby wouldn't lunge again, but the shopkeeper seemed too struck with grief to move.

Hanely came around the table and took Quimby by an arm. 'Help me with him, Hallet.'

Hallet peered at the two men, hesitating, obviously worried what Quimby might do if he got close.

'Move, Hallet, 'fore Bill takes a notion to come checking on the results of the meeting.'

Hallet's gaze darted from Hanely to Quimby, then he came around the table and grabbed Quimby's other arm. The shopkeep made no move to stop him. A blank look washed over his eyes and his steps were mechanical, as they led him from the small room. No one bothered to take his suitcoat from the back of his chair. They walked out into a darkened hallway and made their way to the stairs. They had some trouble negotiating the flight with Quimby's stiff-legged gait, but eventually got him outside into the sultry night air.

Wild screeches and the stench of old

booze, sweat and urine greeted them. A horse came tearing through the wide main street, a cowboy blasting away into the air with his Smith & Wesson and whooping as he thundered past. A number of men hung over rails, vomiting, some falling over into troughs with a splash. One or two might damn well drown, Hanely reckoned, belly turning at the sight of the revelry that had become a nightly affliction since Bill rode in.

From the saloon, a couple blocks down, the off-key clanking of a piano jangled into the night, punctuated by coarse laughter, blistering obscenities and occasional gunshots. Hanely noticed a bargirl with her skirt hoisted up to her thighs, which were wrapped about the waist of a man he recognized as a livery attendant. A married man, vows ignored in the heat of lust. Hanely shifted his gaze, having no desire to watch their public display of wantonness.

Other bargirls staggered about, most of them drunk or high on laudanum, their wares prominently displayed in sateen bodices or peek-a-boo blouses. A few had their tops pulled down completely and were making lewd gestures at cowboys too drunk or too stupid to hold on to their wages.

A brawl erupted across the street over one

19

of the girls. While both men battered each other bloody, she giggled and encouraged the fight.

'Christ, this debauchery sickens me.' Hanely shook his head, trying to focus on the business at hand.

Hallet nodded, but the look in his eyes said different. The little turd was known to sample one of the whores regularly, while his wife made sure the newspaper put up the morning edition.

They made their way across the dusty street towards the newspaper office, half-dragging Quimby now. The man muttered occasionally, tears running down his face, but he made no effort to resist.

The Revelation Pass *Standard* was down the street two blocks and it seemed to take an eternity to reach its front door. The door carried a frosted glass panel with gilt letters proclaiming the newspaper's name. As they drew up, Quimby stared helplessly at the words. Inside, lantern light cast a flickering glow through the large main window, falling across the boardwalk in eerie patterns.

'Be strong, Quimby. Please. For all of us.' Hanely eyed the shopkeep, who nodded, as if in a trance.

Hallet opened the door and they stepped

inside. The redolence of ink and fresh paper rushed into Hanely's nostrils.

A young woman looked up from a Washington Hand Press, at which she was locking wooden letters into type-forms. Her face brightened when she saw her father, an instant later losing its cheerfulness, as she realized that the two other men were holding him upright. Alyssa Quimby had celebrated her eighteenth birthday only a week past. Her large brown eyes and delicate features brought her the attention of many a courting young cowboy, but so far she'd rejected all suitors. Her pa said she was plain picky and the fact had caused him countless nights of lost sleep, Hanely knew. That wouldn't get any better after tonight. A crying shame.

Another woman came from the back room, wiping ink-stained hands on her canvas apron. A heavyset, hard-looking woman just north of her mid-forties, she walked with a hobbling gait, a slight drag to her left leg. Her round face showed a dying bruise on the left cheek and another below her right eye. Bertha Hallet had a habit of 'falling', so Hanely had been told by her newspaperman husband, but the banker suspected different.

The woman's gray-streaked dark hair was yanked back in a tight bun and her eyes flashed them a glare as she paused next to a long table holding rolled-out paper.

'What the devil's going on here?' Her gaze locked on her husband. 'What's wrong with Mr Quimby?'

Alyssa Quimby straightened, concern flooding her eyes. She came up to the three men, peered at her father. 'Pa, what's wrong? What happened to you?'

The shopkeep's eyes focused on his daughter, emotion penetrating the blank look. He stood by his own power and the other men released him. 'I'm ... so sorry ... so sorry...'

Concern changed to worry on Alyssa's face. Her fingers twisted at the ink-stained blouse she wore, eyes widening a notch. 'What is it, Pa? Why are you sorry?'

'Please come with us, Miss Quimby,' Hanely said, having no wish to prolong the necessary and create any kind of a scene. Not that it would matter to anyone in this town, but if the girl put up a fuss it'd only make it harder on all concerned.

'Come with you? Where?' Confusion welled on her features.

'Pastor Bill wishes to see you.' Hanely couldn't even look at her when he said it. Hallet wasn't the only coward in the lot, he reckoned.

The young woman's face hardened. 'Bill? Why? What would he want with me?'

She looked to each man, their faces drawn, somber. Behind her, Bertha Hallet's expression dropped into a mask of defeat.

'You best go with them, girl. It'll only be worse if you give them trouble.' With that the older woman turned and hobbled towards the back room.

Hanely grabbed one of the young woman's arms. Hallet followed suit on the opposite side. Quimby made no move to stop them. He appeared utterly defeated, resigned.

'See here, Mr Hanely! Just what is the meaning of this?' Anger swept aside the young woman's worry.

Hanely frowned. 'Don't make this harder on your pa, Alyssa. Just come with us. Bill has summoned you.'

'Summoned me? What are you talking about? Pa, what are they talking about? Tell me!' Her voice climbed in pitch.

Jacob Quimby's eyes focused on his daughter, and in them was reflected the damnation of a man who was too weak in the soul to save his daughter or himself. 'I'm sorry, sweetie, I truly am. I tried to stop it. I tried. Please forgive me. Please forgive me.'

'Forgive you? What do you mean? Forgive

you for what? I don't understand.'

Hanely gripped his resolve, which he feared would falter if he let her questioning go on any longer. He pulled the young woman towards the door, Hallet taking his cue from the banker and doing the same. Quimby trudged after them as they walked out into the night, a man in a trance, a man burdened with grief and guilt and no chance of redemption.

'Mr Hallet, I insist you tell me the meaning of this!' The young woman struggled but the men were too strong. They pulled her along the boardwalk, her defiance turning to fright.

Hallet gave her a small frown. 'Sorry, Miss Alyssa. It isn't personal, believe me. You're a pretty young gal who didn't take a suitor. Reckon that was your downfall.'

The fear in the girl's eyes swelled into panic. 'You're frightening me, Mr Hallet.'

Hallet looked at her, with a strangely serene expression. 'I don't mean to, Miss Quimby. Truly I don't.' Something in his tone called him a liar and it disgusted Hanely, but not enough to turn them around and let the young woman run from this town, along with her father. He glanced back to see Quimby trudging along behind them, each footfall

24

leaden, forced, driven by some automatic impulse from his benumbed mind.

Drunken cowboys staggered past them, a few making obscene motions at the young woman. Hanely clouted one man whose britches were tangled down around his knees for one of the gestures, feeling only a bit of comfort by the chivalrous display.

A small white church lay ahead, near the end of the main street where it split into a fork. The building was whitewashed and sparkling, a place designed to offer serenity and comfort to the weak and weary. But it did neither. It merely offered damnation and terror. Hanely shuddered as they neared it. The young woman still struggled in his grip, but she had gone silent, and maybe that ate at his nerves even more than her questions.

They dragged her towards the front stairs, noting a man standing near the bottom, smoking a cigarette. The man, a harsh-looking individual with a scar running from his left nostril to his ear, gazed at them and nodded.

Hanely tried not to look at him, instead focusing on getting Alyssa Quimby up the steps, Hallet barely holding up his end. Weak in spirit, weak in body, Hanely reckoned.

They reached the large double doors and

paused. Hallet pushed the left one inward. From within flickering flamelight spilled out across the doorstep, like some sort of welcoming fiery demon.

Hanely heard Quimby utter a small squawk behind them. The shopkeep gave a violent shake of his head. 'I can't, I can't...'

'Stay out here, Quimby,' Hanely said, nodding. 'We'll do what's necessary.'

As they stepped inside, Quimby, half-way up the stairs, leaned over the rail and heaved everything in his belly into the bushes.

The man standing at the bottom of the steps looked up and bellowed a harsh laugh. 'Goddamn, Quimby, you're a weak sonofabitch, ain't ya?'

Quimby's head came up, vomit dripping down his chin, gaze locking on the hardcase with hate. 'Go to hell, Bartlett.'

The man called Bartlett eyed him, looking as if he might charge up the steps and beat the hell out of Quimby. He shrugged after a moment, laughed again, then wandered around to the back of the church.

Quimby pushed himself away from the rail.

Inside, Hanely and Hallet dragged the young woman through an anteroom that stank of must and old books. The place gave Hanely the creeps. He reckoned churches

26

always had and he damn sure didn't belong in one now, especially this one. This one was tainted, procured by the Devil, who likely already had Hanely's soul bought and branded.

The interior was gloomy, choked with shadows and amber lantern-glow. A handful of pews lined each side of a short aisle. Amber glass windows ran the length of each side, smaller clear panes at the front.

On the altar stood a man who might well have been Old Nick himself, in Hanely's estimation. Gaunt face and drawn features highlighted by twin burning candlesticks to each side, his nearly colorless eyes fixed intently upon them as they approached. Dressed in black, with a white clerical collar, he stood with clasped bony hands, jutting Adam's apple bobbing as if by some nervous impulse. To either side of the man stood hardcases, deacons, Bill liked to call them, but hardcases all the same. Their gazes raked the girl with barely restrained lust.

The expression on the gaunt man's face remained placid, yet vile in a way that Hanely would be hard-pressed to describe. It was the look of a spider eyeing a plump fly caught in its web; that was the best description Hanely could put to it.

'You are late, Brother Hanely.' The man's voice was controlled, airy, carrying a hint of accusation.

'It was Quimby's daughter...' Hanely said, as if that offered an excuse that would prove acceptable to a man such as the one standing before him.

The man's tongue poked at the inside of his cheek. His pale eyes shifted to the girl.

He stepped down from the altar, coming up to her. 'Ah, Miss Alyssa Quimby. I have long prayed for your soul to bless my humble dwelling.' His thin hand drifted up, the back of his fingers stroking her cheek. 'Such a pretty young thing, too.'

'Jesus, Bill, this is hard enough. You don't have to talk that way.' It slipped out, whether through fear or some last-minute spark of courage, before Hanely could stop it.

Bill's gaze locked on the banker. 'My dear Brother Hanely, still your tongue in the Lord's house. His righteous sword is swift in its judgment. Who are we to question His infinite wisdom and workings?'

Hanely had no idea what the devil the man was talking about but it came with a clear tone of threat. The banker knew better than to push his luck any further. He would do what he had done a score of times before

– go home and drink himself into a state of oblivion where he couldn't feel guilt and disgust.

'What do you want with me, Reverend?' Alyssa Quimby asked, eyes frightened but defiant again.

'Want, my dear?' The man's voice remained a steady drone, counterfeit. Hanely reckoned the man was plumb insane or had picked up the silly affectation from one of those damn dime novels that passed as entertainment these days. He was no preacher, that was for damn sure. 'Why, I want nothing from you. Nothing at all. But another man ... ah, maybe it's better that you learn that for yourself. Take her...' He ducked his chin towards a back door, to the left of the altar. The two hardcases stepped forward and grabbed the girl's arms, jerking her away from Hanely and Hallet. Hallet suddenly looked more shaken than he had all night, but still strangely gleeful. Hanely struggled to swallow the bile surging into his throat. He would be joining Quimby in heaving his innards before the night was through.

Alyssa Quimby started screaming and struggling. Any measure of composure fled from her and she tried to pull her arms free of the hardcases' grip. One of the men clouted her full across the face. Her head rocked and blood spattered from her mashed lips. She collapsed and they dragged her to the door at the back, disappearing into a back room.

A yell came from the front of the church. The three men turned to see Quimby staggering up the aisle, his face sunken and twisted with grief. He reached the three, collapsing to his knees before the gaunt preacher.

'Please...' His voice quaked, lips trembling, sweat streaming down his face. 'Please, let me have her back. She's my daughter. My only child. My wife's passed. She's all I have.'

Pastor Bill gazed down at him, a look of cold sympathy on his face Hanely knew was faked. 'Why, Brother Quimby, you should be honored. She's going to do the Lord's work. He watches over this town, you know. And I watch over His flock. It is the only way.'

'Please, have mercy...' Quimby shook his head. 'You can't take her.'

Pastor Bill's features tightened. 'But I can. Her name was drawn, was it not? After last night's mistake you should feel blessed that the Almighty hasn't instructed me to strike you down. Your daughter is ample compensation, and such a small price to pay for the serenity enjoyed by this town.'

'You bastard!' Quimby screamed the words, suddenly grabbing a handful of the pastor's trouser-leg. 'Give me back my daughter, you sonofabitch!'

A flash of black fire ignited in the preacher's pale eyes. His knee jerked up, its bony point smashing into Quimby's chin. Quimby's teeth clacked together and blood sprayed from his lips. Pastor Bill hoisted his leg a second time, foot sweeping around and colliding with Quimby's jaw. The shopkeep toppled backwards, hit the aisle floor with a heavy thud and lay groaning.

Pastor Bill backed away, gazed at the other men, his face momentarily twisted with something Hanely had never before witnessed on another human being: utter hatred, contempt. Not a lick of compassion. If there was such a thing as pure evil, the man exemplified it.

'Get him out of my sight.' Bill's voice came hard and low, pregnant with barely restrained fury.

Hanely nodded. Hallet quickly followed the banker's direction as he bent and helped Quimby to his feet. Quimby muttered through his teeth, a liquid sound. Blood bubbled from his nose and mouth. They half-dragged, half-walked him down the aisle to the door. Hanely refused to glance back, knowing the little bastard's eyes were drilling into their backs. Alyssa Quimby was now dead to the world for all intents. She would never be seen again; that much he knew from the twenty-odd other women they'd brought to Pastor Bill. What he did with them Hanely had no idea and no desire to learn. Only one had returned, that one a mistake left hanging as a gruesome reminder to be more careful in future lotteries.

Insane? Yes, the man was insane. But deadly. And, as far as Hanely was concerned, all-powerful.

CHAPTER TWO

Her body was the last thing Jim Hannigan expected to find the moment he reached Revelation Pass, Colorado. Christ, it was a simple runaway case, nothing dangerous, nothing ... lethal. Find her, fetch her and haul her back to her pa, fifty miles north in Wolf's Bend. Sixteen-year-old gals sometimes took a notion to be headstrong and go chasin' some fool will-'o-the-wisp.

Amy Breck had ridden away from the family farm early one morning three weeks ago with a hare-brained notion that she was old enough to make her own way in a man's world and show her pa a thing or two about a woman's role in a fast-changing West. Stubborn, but iron-willed, much like her old man – a cattle-magnate with more money than time for raisin' a daughter – Amy Breck was a girl who'd return home only after she reached her goals and set the world on its head.

But she would never return home. Her father's life would be flipped upside down, true enough, but not for the reasons she'd promised him.

Jim Hannigan let out a strangled sound of disgust. Bitter sorrow burned in his belly. He tugged on the reins of the big roan beneath him, slowing it to a halt, as he peered up at the body swaying from the limb of a cottonwood. The woods thinned here, opening into stands of aspen and spruce, pine and ash. Twenty feet on, where the trail sloped towards the town, a handful of paces from the death tree, a weathered board nailed to a post read: REVELATION PASS POPULATION SAVED.

Revelation Pass? That wasn't right, was it? Centerville was, or at least had been, the name of this town last time Jim passed through a couple – three years back. An out-of-the-way cowtown from which Amy Breck had telegraphed her pa only a few days before, assuring him she was all right and would write again soon. She had called the town Centerville in her post, the way it was labeled on old maps of the area, told her pa she had settled in and taken a job with the dressmaker. Had she deliberately used the former name to throw her father off? She hadn't thought it out, if that were the case. The town was still Centerville, no matter when its name changed, easy enough to locate.

Hannigan drew a deep breath of heated air. Sweat trickled down his lined but handsome face. His hazel eyes narrowed. Shifting his rangy frame in the saddle, he heeled the horse to the side of the trail. He dismounted, tethered the roan to a branch and approached the swaying corpse.

Disgust twisted in his belly and he suppressed a shudder, despite the heat.

The sun and carrion-feeders had played hell with the remains but the gored features were still recognizable. The skirt and blouse were shredded in places; patches of flesh, some torn clean to the bone by scavengers, showed through. Maggots crawled over the young woman's corpse. The stench of rotting flesh brought a burst of nausea to his belly and it was all he could do not to lean over and hurl his breakfast of jerky and Arbuckle's into the bushes. In all his years manhunting he'd never felt so sickened by the sight of a body. Of course, most bodies he encountered came courtesy of his ivory-gripped Peacemaker, but he had seen some grisly things in his career.

He wasn't a religious man, but he whispered a prayer, then pulled the Bowie knife from his boot-sheath. Wrapping one arm around the girl's waist, he sliced through the rope at the back of her neck. Her lifeless form fell across his shoulder and he quickly lowered her to the ground, a chill riding his spine as he brushed worms from his shirt.

Sheathing the knife, he returned to his horse and pulled a rolled blanket from his gear, then slung it over a shoulder. Fishing through a saddle-bag, he located a tintype before going back to the corpse. Squatting, he tossed the blanket beside the girl. Comparing the face on the picture with that of the body, he confirmed what he already knew.

'Jesus, this ain't the way it was s'posed to turn out,' he muttered, a great wave of sorrow flooding his soul. How the hell was he going to tell a worried father that he had located his wayward daughter hanging from a tree? How was he going to tell the man his pride and joy would never grace another dinner table or fill a house with the lilt of her laughter?

Judas Priest, sometimes manhunting was a damned ugly business. This once he thought he'd taken an easy case, with virtually no danger element, in order to protect someone he cared about, another young woman whom the past couple months had brought ever closer to him. She wouldn't have wanted that protection, but he reckoned he'd outfoxed her. He should have known it would bite him in the backside.

He hung his head a moment. 'Men don't hire you for justice; they hire you for vengeance. Ain't that what you always say? No free rides in this world, Hannigan.'

Whether Jeremy Breck wanted to hire Hannigan to track his daughter's killer or not, he vowed right then to punish whoever had done this.

Rising, he returned to his horse and stuffed the tintype into a saddle-bag. Sweat dripped down his chest with the sensation of ants crawling over his flesh. He lifted his Stetson, mopped his brow with a forearm.

Who could have done such a thing? Why? She'd been alive only a few days ago and the corpse obviously hadn't been hanging there long enough for the buzzards to strip it completely.

His gaze drifted up, centering on the town, which rippled under shimmering heat waves rising from the ground. Was her killer in that town? Or had he – assuming it was a man – merely been passing through, by now long gone? Why hadn't anyone from the town noticed the body, cut it down? He aimed to find out, and that meant letting wheels already in motion keep turning, at least for the time being.

He returned to the corpse, squatting, then unrolling the blanket. With gloved hands he brushed away as many of the maggots as he could before rolling the girl onto the blanket. He wrapped her within, straightened. With a grunt he heaved her body over a shoulder, carried her back to his roan. As if placing a baby in its crib, he draped her over the saddle.

Untethering the roan, he gripped the reins and led the horse back onto the trail. He started walking towards the town. Nerves buzzing, a strange apprehension wandered through him he couldn't account for. Years of experience had imbued him with an almost sixth sense when it came to cases, and this one was setting off warning-bells as strong as any he'd ever felt.

As he entered the town his gaze roved over the wide main street. The town appeared utterly serene. He noted folks sweeping down the boardwalks, others polishing windows and lanterns. Their eyes carried a glazed look. A woman garbed in a yellow day dress, twirling a frill-edged parasol, gazed at him as she passed, a lifeless smile turning her lips.

'Good day, stranger,' she said, her look slightly coy, oblivious to the body draped over his saddle. She went on her way and others tipped their hats to him as he walked along the street. Women smiled, or turned demurely away, while men beamed friendly grins that somehow fell short of the mark.

'What the hell?' he whispered. He'd spent a considerable amount of time in any number of cowtowns across the West, some friendly, some downright lawless, but none that impressed him as so utterly ... *vacant* was the only word he could put to it. It wasn't the reception he would have expected upon walking into a town with a body slung over his saddle.

He stopped, gazing about, puzzled. Spotting a man stepping from the general store, he stepped towards him, guiding the roan sideways.

'You...' He ducked his chin at the man, who looked up.

For an instant Hannigan noted an expression in the man's eyes that was anything but vacant when the fellow's gaze focused on the corpse. Fear. Not surprise at the sight, not repulsion, but unadulterated fear. The man had mutton-chop side-whiskers and a brocade vest, looked to be somewhere in his forties, maybe early fifties. The fellow's expression shifted, but not enough to disguise completely the alarm behind his eyes.

'Welcome to Revelation Pass, sir,' the man said, voice unsteady.

'Who's your law here?' Hannigan's gaze locked with the man's.

'We have no law here. Revelation Pass is a free town, welcome to all.'

'What the hell you mean, no law? How do you keep bandits from running wild?'

The man shifted feet, swallowed hard. 'Bandits don't come here. Only decent folk

39

live in Revelation Pass.'

Hannigan caught something else under-lying the man's words, but damned if he knew what it was. The fellow was lying, of that he felt certain, but about what, and why?

'You got a funeral man? I take it folks don't live forever in Revelation Pass.'

The man's eyes darted. 'Funeral man?' His face went a shade paler. Hannigan studied him, noting that the man seemed on the verge of coming apart, though he was doing his best to present a confident air. Something ate at this man, something too powerful for him to come to grips with. But did it have anything to do with the body on Hannigan's saddle, or were they personal demons?

'Your welcoming little town usually hang a corpse out as a signpost, Mr...?'

The man's gaze flicked to the blanket-covered form, then back to Hannigan. Han-nigan saw the man's knees nearly buckle.

A door opened across the street and a man in a three-piece suit with a gold watch-chain hanging from the vest stepped out onto the boardwalk. His lips set into a firm line beneath his handlebar mustache. A moment later, he came towards Hannigan.

'Welcome to Revelation Pass, my good

man,' said the man. 'I'm Bertrim Hanely, bank manager and town mayor. I see you've met Quimby, the general store owner.'

The banker's voice carried an ingratiating quality that Hannigan little cared for, but the fellow was built of sturdier stuff than the shopkeep, Quimby. Hannigan bet the banker had been watching them the entire time and had stepped in just as Quimby started to falter. But why? Were they hiding something? Did they know full well how the corpse had come to be hanging outside their town?

'Thought this town was named Centerville.' Hannigan's gaze locked with the banker's.

Hanely nodded. 'Used to be, up till I reckon going on twenty months now. We decided Centerville wasn't distinct enough, didn't say what we wanted it to say.'

Hannigan glanced along the street at the folks strolling about as if in a trance. His gaze went back to Hanely. 'And Revelation Pass says what?'

The man grinned, smug, but likely intended to be disarming. 'Why, my fellow, Revelation Pass is a haven in a Wild West, a place of respite, welcoming to all.'

Hannigan's eyes cut to the blanket-covered corpse, then back to Hanely. 'Reckon she

41

wouldn't agree.'

Hanely glanced at the blanket and for the first time Hannigan saw nervousness dance in the man's eyes.

'Nothing like this has ever occurred in this town, my fellow, I assure you.' Hanely kept his voice steady, regained his composure.

Hannigan offered a wan smile. 'Nothing like what, Mr Hanely?'

Hanely flinched, knowing damned well he'd just been caught in his words. 'I ... don't know what you mean, sir.' No confidence came with his tone this time.

'Reckon you know exactly what I mean. I didn't tell you what happened to this girl. You knew it already, didn't you?'

'I ... no, certainly not. I ... I just figured something mighty awful must have occurred for you to be bringing her back here wrapped in a blanket.' Hanely's voice took on more strength as he talked but Hannigan heard a lie all the same.

A block down another door opened, this one belonging to the local newspaper. Hannigan saw a mousy little *hombre* step out onto the boardwalk, gaze locked on the three of them. The man hesitated, then strolled towards them.

'Mr Hallet, the newspaper owner,' Hanely

said, as the man reached them.

'You three the welcoming committee?' Hannigan asked.

Hanely grimaced. 'We are the town governing committee – Mr Quimby, Mr Hallet and myself. We have no law here.'

Hannigan nodded. 'So I've been told. Just what *do* you have here, Mr Hanely? What I'm seein' so far I ain't likin' in the least.'

'Who are you, my fellow?' Hanely's face pinched, reddened a hint.

'Name's Hannigan. I came here to your town looking for a man's daughter.' He glanced at the blanketed form. 'Reckon I found her.'

'Perhaps it would best if you moved on, then,' Hallet said, a slight hitch in his voice.

Hannigan eyed him. 'Welcome wore out damned fast, didn't it?'

'Not at all.' Hanely shook his head. 'It's just that we aren't used to problems here. We run a peaceful town.'

Hannigan's irritation stepped up a notch. 'Mr Hanely, I ain't a particularly patient man, especially when I'm saddled with the responsibility of telling a rancher that his daughter, whom I was sent to escort home, will be riding back in a box instead of on a horse. You best damned tell me what you

43

know about this poor girl hanging from a cottonwood before my temper goes off a hair before my gun.'

Hanely shifted feet, glanced at Quimby, then Hallet. 'We know nothing of this girl, sir. It is a complete shock to us, I assure you, and most ... unfortunate.'

'She was a stranger anyways, didn't belong here,' Hallet said, shaking his head. 'She should have been more careful.'

'Shut up, Hallet,' Hanely said, catching the same thing Hannigan did.

Hannigan's gaze settled on Hallet. 'Reckon that makes somebody here a liar, Hallet ... 'less you can see through wool.'

Hallet licked his lips, eyes widening slightly, a panicked look igniting within them.

'I'm sure what Mr Hallet was trying to say was, none of our girls are missing, so it must be a stranger...' The voice was unnaturally level and came from a spot just up a few steps from Quimby. A man had come up, damned quietlike in Hannigan's estimation. He wore a dark suit with a white collar. A man of the cloth, with a gaunt face and dark half-circles nesting below nearly colorless eyes. He reminded Hannigan of a spider somehow, thin flesh stretched taut over sharp bone and a large head.

With his approach Quimby's face washed white and for a moment Hannigan thought the man might pitch sideways and faint dead away.

The other two looked suddenly jittery, but to a lesser degree than the shopkeep.

'You are?' Hannigan asked.

The man smiled, a spider smile, and spread his hands in an exaggerated gesture. 'I am a vessel of the Light of the World, sir, a humble messenger.'

Hannigan was starting to wonder whether the whole damn town was just plain loco. 'I figured that out from the collar.' His eyes narrowed, a sudden twinge of familiarity taking him. 'We met somewhere before?'

The man's spider smile widened and he took a step closer. He interlaced his fingers. 'I am certain that if we had I would remember you, sir. You appear to be a man of the gun. Am I not right?'

Hannigan nodded. 'Close enough. Right now I got a body on my horse and damned little co-operation from these three here. Maybe you'd care to be more helpful, seeing as how you do the Lord's work an' all?'

The man came down three stairs onto the street. His gaze traveled to the blanket-wrapped form and he shook his head, a look of sadness pinching his features like a drawstring. 'Such a sad thing, isn't it, when a life is cut short before its time?'

Hannigan cocked an eyebrow. 'You tellin' me you know her?'

The pastor shook his head. 'She was one of God's children, was she not? She is our sister, a lost soul, perhaps.'

Hannigan's nerves cinched another notch. He was getting the run-around. 'I'll say this once and I best get a straight answer out of one of you. I was sent here to fetch Amy Breck and bring her home to her father. I found her hanging outside your town. That's her body in the blanket, but I got a notion one or maybe even all of you already know that.'

'Then your mission here is finished, yes?' the preacher said.

Hannigan's eyes locked with the man's. 'Hell it is. I aim to find out why this girl is dead in your supposedly peaceful little town, reverend, or whatever you are.'

'I am Pastor Bill.' The man's smile took on the genuineness of a whore's laugh. 'This is my town, its people my flock. None of them would harm a soul, I assure you.'

'You'll forgive me if I hold onto my doubts?' Hannigan kept the man's gaze.

Something flickered deep within the pastor's colorless eyes, but Hannigan couldn't be certain what it was. The only thing he would have wagered was that it was anything but saintly.

'Please express my condolences to her father...' Was there a note of sarcasm in the preacher's tone? Hannigan might have bet on that, too.

Quimby suddenly seemed to lose all the strength in his legs and half-stumbled sideways, where he gripped a supporting beam to hold himself up. His fingernails dug deep into the wood. Sweat streamed down his face now, drenching his collar. His eyes carried a distant look and his lips drained bone white.

'Mr Quimby suffers from the Devil's affliction,' Pastor Bill said, his voice remaining a drone. 'We will chase the Dark One from him with a few more Sundays in the Lord's house, I am certain.'

Hannigan had little desire to ask the man what the hell he was talking about, but Quimby and the others obviously took some meaning out of the words.

'Where's the funeral man?' Hannigan's gaze swept over the four men. 'I best not get a crooked answer.'

Hanely and Hallet eyed each other, then

the pastor.

'Tell the good man where Jackman's place is, Mr Hanely. We must show a stranger the same hospitality we would show a loved one. It is the Lord's way.'

Hanely cleared his throat. 'Four blocks down, on the right.'

Hannigan nodded. 'Wish I could say I was obliged, but since that's the first straight answer any of you have given me you'll forgive my lack of gratitude.'

'All is forgiven in Revelation Pass, stranger.' Pastor Bill smiled the spider smile again.

Hannigan had a healthy urge to jam a fist down his throat. 'Not all...' He looked at the bundled form on his horse.

'"Vengeance is mine, sayeth the Lord".' The preacher's tone carried a harder edge this time and Hannigan almost smiled.

'Reckon this time He'll be only too happy to share.' He held the man's colorless eyes, neither averting. 'Now suppose you tell me where the telegraph office is?'

A slight gasp came from Quimby and Hallet said quickly: 'We ain't got one. Don't need it.'

Hannigan cocked an eyebrow. 'Makes it damn peculiar, then, that this girl sent her pa a message from one in this town just a

48

few days ago. It get up and walk off?'

All four remained silent and Hannigan shook his head. He grabbed the reins of his horse, then turned to look back at them. 'Reckon I'll be seein' each of you again right soon. You best get your stories straight 'fore I do.'

He walked away, feeling them staring after him. His gaze shifted from side to side, folks smiling vacantly as he passed. Windows sparkled with sunlight and wherever there was metal it gleamed, highly polished. He reckoned he'd never seen a town so clean, so … sterile? That was as good a word as any. But just what lay beneath the luster?

If the dead girl were any indication, something dark, something unlike anything he'd ever encountered.

He spotted a boarded-up building to his left, noting the word *marshal* lettered in gold across the window. No law now, but there had been in the past. What had happened to it, to this town?

More questions added to a growing list. Across the street he saw a telegraph office, confirming Hallet's lie. He would have to send Breck a note about his daughter, though damned if he had any taste for it. He would also inform the man that he was staying on

49

the case until he discovered her killer.

A rumble pulled him from his thoughts. A stage came from the opposite direction, iron tires raising clouds of dust. The contraption rattled by him and he spotted a pretty blonde peering from the cab window. A slight smile turned her lips as she noticed him and he tipped a finger to his hat.

A sudden jolt of apprehension rose within him at the thought of the young woman arriving in this town with a murderer running loose. He didn't care a lick for the feeling and it wasn't one he was used to. But for the moment there was nothing he could do about it. It was one of the many uncomfortable emotions he'd been plagued with over the past couple months. He wished he didn't know why.

CHAPTER THREE

After the stage came to a halt Hannah Garret opened the cab door and stepped out into the blistering heat. She tugged on her blue day-dress's matching coat and snapped open her fan with an arrogant flare. 'Dreadful heat, perfectly dreadful,' she said in an annoyed Southern drawl loud enough for the driver to hear. She reckoned she'd irritated him sufficiently over the past few miles and wasn't about to let up now that she'd reached her destination.

With a sigh she folded the fan and tucked it into a pocket. She fluffed the bottom of her blond locks, worn with a fringe and piled high beneath a 'Rubens' hat. The interior of the cab had been sweltering, the heat reddening her olive cheeks and making her perspire to a point where she was nearly swimming beneath her dress. She silently cursed the choice of costume. On top of everything, her tailbone ached, her legs felt stiff and her disposition had taken a southern turn roughly five miles back. With a sharp 'hmmph' she jutted her nose into the air and offered the driver, who was climbing from the seat, a castigating glare for her extreme displeasure with hard seats, cramped conditions and jarring ride.

The driver peered at her and shrugged. 'Hell, you want luxury, hire a Concord.'

She cocked an eyebrow and plucked at the cuff on her left wrist. 'I will thank you not to use such coarse language around me, suh. You should know better when in the presence of a lady.' She emphasized the proclamation with a curt nod and a narrowing of her mahogany eyes.

The driver, an unshaven man with a sweat-soaked shirt and part of an earlobe missing, smirked, spat, then yanked her portmanteau from the top of the carriage and tossed it to the ground at her feet. 'There's yer belongin's. Can't say I'm all-fired unhappy to be rid of ya.'

Her brow crinkled indignantly. '*Well*, certainly you have not an ounce of breeding, suh. I do declare, your parents would be downright ashamed to see the crass approximation of a human being you have turned out to be.' She put as much spite into her words as she could, the soft Georgian accent overlaying a hint of Mexican spice in her tone.

'My parents were coyotes.' The driver's gaze raked her modest bosom and womanly curves. Then he shook his head. 'Hell, wouldn't be worth puttin' up with the attitude.'

She stamped a foot and pressed her lips into an annoyed line. 'Well, I have never been treated with such disrespect in all my days. I most certainly hope all men of the West are not of your low bearing. I shan't long remain in this Territory if that is the case.'

He scoffed and gave her a look that said he knew some secret he wasn't about to tell, because it provided him perverse enjoyment. 'Reckon you'll find worse than me, ma'am. West eats you prissy types for breakfast and spits you out a'cause your meat's too stringy.'

She worked her expression into an insulted glare. 'I assure you, I can acquit myself just fine. You had just better be more obliging when it comes time for me to depart this town, suh. I expect better treatment on my return to the East.'

He eyed her with the secret expression again and she wondered what lay behind his bloodshot eyes. 'Won't be a return trip, ma'am. Young gals like yourself, they only come into Revelation Pass. They don't leave it.'

With these words he turned, slammed the cab door, then climbed back up into the driver's seat. He didn't look back as he snapped the reins and sent the team charging forward. The iron tires churned up a cloud of dust. With a gloved hand she fanned it away from her face, coughing.

'We'll see about that, mister,' she said, voice hardening as she watched the stage head for the end of town. What had the driver meant by his cryptic statement? Revelation Pass was just another Western town, much like a hundred others scattered across the Territory. Everything routine, though immeasurably vulgar to a woman of such fine breeding as Hannah Garret.

She peered at the portmanteau before her in the dust and sighed, wondering how far she'd have to carry it to a hotel. Wasn't like it didn't weigh half as much as she did.

With sigh, she hoisted it and stepped onto the boardwalk, scanning the town in both directions. Funny, everything appeared rather spotless for a cowtown. Folks wandered along the boardwalks like drones, odd little smiles glued to their faces. Well, not really smiles. More like the expression on wooden puppets.

'Welcome to Revelation Pass, miss,' a man passing her said, tipping his hat. His smile widened and nearly swallowed his face but it still looked strained. She gave him a proper Southern gal curtsy.

Making her way along the boardwalk, she made note of the locations of various businesses and the town's Y-like layout. Buildings of clapboard, shiplap, some brick. She spotted a boarded-up marshal's office, bank and general store, a closed saloon. Her gaze settled on the window of the newspaper office directly to her left. Stopping, she focused on the small sign propped in the window. Scrawled on the paper in poor handwriting it read: HELP WANTED. She studied it a moment, debating something, then decided she liked the idea. It was just the position that might serve her well during the day.

Her carriage relaxed a bit and she lowered her chin just a notch. Her gloved fingers went to her hair, pulling a pin from either side to let wisps of blond corkscrew down beside her high cheek-bones. She casually dropped the pins onto the boardwalk. Wouldn't do to appear too prissy when applying for a job, would it?

A voice came from behind her and she turned, pulled from her thoughts. A young woman in a blue gingham dress held out the pins she had tossed away. 'I believe you dropped these, miss. We pride ourselves on cleanliness in this town.' A scolding came with the soft voice.

'What?' She stared at the auburn-haired young woman in surprise.

'We don't cotton to throwing items on the ground here. We have laws against such things. Pastor Bill insists cleanliness is next to Godliness.' The girl thrust her hand further forward.

Hannah took the pins and deposited them in a pocket. 'I beg your pardon.' She wasn't quite sure what else to say.

'You are a stranger here, so you could not have known.' The girl smiled and something came with the expression, Hannah didn't much care for. Mechanical, but tinged with that same secretive thing the stage-driver had exhibited.

'My name is Hannah Garret. I have only just arrived. I plan to apply for the position at the newspaper advertised in the window.' She ducked her chin at the newspaper office.

The girl's smile didn't change. 'Welcome to Revelation Pass, Miss Garret. You are required to register with the mayor within twenty-four hours of your arrival. He is also the bank-man, so you will have no trouble finding him. I'm sure you will enjoy your stay.' The girl curtsied and strode away.

Hannah stared after her. 'Register?' she mumbled, suddenly more puzzled than ever.

Noticing that her shoulder and arm were beginning to ache from the weight of the portmanteau, she shook off her bewilderment and went to the newspaper-office door.

She stepped inside, set the suitcase on the

floor and massaged her forearm. The redolence of ink and the tang of fresh paper assailed her nostrils. The clatter of a press came to a halt. A smallish man with a face like an ugly mouse peered up at her, a peculiar smile coming onto his features. She had been in Revelation Pass no more than a few moments but already she was sick of that expression. The whole place was on some sort of sour happy-juice, way it looked.

From the back came a heavyset woman with the exact opposite expression. The woman twisted at her apron. The small man stood, came towards her, eagerness in his eyes.

'Why, my fine young lady, what may I do for you?'

Hannah smiled and tried to look more innocent than uppity. If she pegged this fellow right, she'd have him dancing 'round her every word in no time.

'Why, I saw the sign in your window, suh, and I find myself qualified highly for any position you might offer.' She made sure he didn't miss the double meaning to her words.

The man grinned, a lewd light sparking in his eyes. 'Do I detect an accent, Miss–'

'Garret. Hannah Garret, and I do declare you most certainly do, kind suh. Georgia peach, born and bred.' She gave him a demure cocking of her head and placed her splayed fingers innocently over her bosom.

'Always wanted to visit the East myself, yes, I did. Always wanted to visit. And we certainly need the help. You have writing skills, yes? Of course you do. Intelligent woman like yourself. Some office work, too.'

The heavyset woman cleared her throat with more than a little disapproval aimed at the gushing mouse of a man. The woman ran her gaze up and down Hannah, apparently unimpressed. 'You don't look like reporter material to me. Why don't you just take my advice and ride on to the next town.'

'Why, Bertha,' said the man, 'that's no way to treat a guest in our town. You know what Pastor Bill always says, a stranger is just a friend we ain't got to know yet.'

'Pastor Bill...' The woman frowned, the lines of her face prematurely aging her and emphasizing the shadows of a bruise on her cheek.

The mousy man's expression darkened a notch. 'Bertha, you know better...'

The heavyset woman looked away, something passing between them Hannah couldn't even guess at.

'Please, Miss Garret – it is Miss, isn't it?'

The man rubbed his hands together with a sandpaper sound.

She gave him a demure look. 'Why, sadly, yes. Alas I have had no suitors, suh. I wonder if men are simply afraid of little old me.'

'Oh, my, no, I'm sure it's just as Pastor Bills says, there's a right one for everyone, yes, indeed, there is. A right one for everyone.'

Hannah jotted a couple instant impressions in her mind. One, whoever this Pastor Bill was, he had considerable influence in this town. Two, she concluded that this newspaperman was an idiot, and likely stepping out on his wife, who was the heavyset woman, judging from the matching bands on their fingers. Why else would he ask about her suitor status?

'I assure you my credentials come from the finest Georgian university and can be forwarded upon notice, suh,' she said, shifting the subject.

He beamed and she resisted the urge to slap the expression off his face. Instead she gave him a warm smile and pushed her bosom out.

'Oh, no need, no need. As it is, the young lady who worked here before found ... alternate employment. I am sure you'll fill the position nicely. I am Mr Hallet, owner of this fine paper.'

'A pleasure, suh.' She batted eyelashes, hoping she wasn't overdoing the charm, but the man didn't impress her as bright enough to pick up on the deception. How he'd ever managed a newspaper was beyond her. Likely his wife had much to do with that.

'How soon do you think you can start, Miss Garret?'

'Why, near immediately, suh. I simply need to establish myself at one of your fine hostelries and rest a bit from my long journey. I declare, the trip was simply dreadful.'

'Only one hotel in Revelation Pass, Miss Garret. Just down four blocks. I'm sure you'll find the accommodations to your liking. You come back here tomorrow morning and we'll get you started.'

'Shouldn't we check on her credentials?' Bertha asked, but Hallet gave her a cross look and her frown deepened. She went silent.

'As I was saying. You come by tomorrow morning.' He took her hand in his damp palms, and she resisted the urge to pull it free and kept the repulsion off her face.

'Thank you kindly, suh. I look forward to...' Hannah smiled. 'Beginning a new life.'

She wouldn't have been surprised to see

drool slither out of Hallet's mouth, but instead he stood grinning foolishly at her. She almost laughed. There were times she swore she could make a man do anything she wanted. Well, with the exception of one man...

Pulling her hand loose, she went to her portmanteau and bent to pick it up, then looked back to Hallet, who hadn't taken his eyes off her figure. 'Oh, a young woman on the street mentioned something about registering. What is that about?'

Hallet nodded. 'Why, yes, with the mayor, Bertrim Hanely. See, Revelation Pass is a virtuous town, Miss Garret.'

'During the day, at any rate,' muttered Bertha. Hallet flashed her a look.

'As I was saying, Revelation Pass is a virtuous town and we try very hard to keep undesirables out. We require all strangers to register.'

'I see.' Hannah nodded, wondering just how that would keep an outlaw from shooting him through the head the moment he supplied that edict. 'Much obliged, as they say here in the West, suh.'

Hallet preened his hair and stuck out his bony chest. 'I am sure your stay in Revelation Pass will prove very rewarding, Miss

Garret. Very rewarding.'

With a wink, she stepped outside. Uttering an uneasy laugh, she started down the board-walk towards the hotel, unable to shake a sudden notion this town was hiding something. She couldn't put her finger on anything; it was only a feeling at this point. But her feelings were seldom wrong.

She sighed. She was exhausted, damp with perspiration and feeling a little filthy after meeting Hallet. She suddenly wanted nothing more than a cool bath and feather bed. But that wasn't on the horizon. She had more work to do.

Jim Hannigan came out of the telegraph office, Stetson in hand and lead in his belly. He could imagine how Jeremy Breck would take the news of his daughter's death. Shock, grief, anger. Then the emotion that Jim Hannigan understood better than anyone: the craving for vengeance.

He had left the body at the funeral man's, instructing the owner to prepare the corpse for shipment to Wolf's Bend. The arrangements would be up to Breck; the mission was in Jim Hannigan's hands.

It made no sense. The girl should have been alive, on her way back to Breck, likely kicking and screaming, Hannigan as her escort. Some twist of fate had intervened, something deadly and perhaps stitched into the fabric of this outwardly peaceful cowtown.

Peaceful. Was that what the town was? Or was that a façade? Did something darker lurk here? The notion that the killing was random no longer remained, not after the peculiar behavior exhibited by those four men he'd met earlier. The killer was here still, in his estimation; the reason was here.

Where to start? One of the four men? He felt damn sure one or all of the three businessmen, maybe even the preacher, had known that girl was hanging at the edge of town. In itself that wasn't a hanging offense or provable, unless one of them talked and laid blame.

Of the four, he pinpointed Quimby as the most likely to break. The man had some demon breathing down his back. Maybe that was the first order of business. The other two appeared to be made of stronger stuff, and the pastor...

Hell, he had a hard time figuring just what that fellow was up to. A dime-novel preacher, he reckoned, but was that all? Hannigan had taken an immediate aversion to the fellow, and something about him looked vaguely familiar. Where had he seen him before? Try as he might he couldn't force a time or place of meeting from his memory. Maybe the man just resembled someone he'd met somewhere, sometime. Over the course of his career as a manhunter, Hannigan had encountered scores of folks. After a spell their faces all blended together.

As he strolled along the boardwalk folks passed by, smiling their peculiar smiles, tipping their hats. Women curtsied. He'd never seen the likes. The West about these parts wasn't particularly known for its etiquette, yet this town ... this town might have stepped from some storybook.

A door rattled open behind him and he turned to see a young woman stepping from the newspaper office. His brow creased and he stopped, then backed to the corner of a shop and leaned against the building. He eyed the woman, the same one he had seen arriving on the stage. She came towards him, a portmanteau in one hand, a prissy expression on her face.

He smiled and winked, placing his hat on his head. 'Help you with that, ma'am?' He ducked his chin at the suitcase.

The woman stopped, chin tilting up, a look of annoyance replacing the prissy expression. 'I can manage perfectly fine on my own, thank you, suh.'

'I reckon you can. Just figured maybe you were new in this town and since I am too...' He gave her a grin that carried more than a simple welcome. She was right pretty with that tight dress and blond hair. Enough to make any man stutter in his step.

She cast him an indignant glare. 'You are gazing upon me improperly, suh. This is a respectable town and I am a woman of fine breeding. I am quite certain the likes of you has nothing better to do than gaze lasciviously upon young women, but I beseech you to show proper respect when addressing me.'

Hannigan almost laughed, but from the corner of his eye he noticed that Hanely had stepped from the bank onto the opposite boardwalk, and was gazing directly towards them. The young woman seemed to notice Hannigan's attention shifting to the banker. She suddenly slapped him across the face. Hannigan's teeth clacked and the sting of her hand rang through his cheek. He couldn't figure out whether he was more shocked or p-o'd at the strike.

'What the hell?' he blurted.

She glared. 'If there is anything I hate more, suh, than being rudely looked upon, it is not being looked upon at all!' She jutted her nose into the air and proceeded past him in a huff.

Hannigan rubbed his face. Across the street Hanely might have smiled but he wasn't certain. The banker disappeared back into the building after watching the young woman enter the hotel a couple blocks down.

Hannigan shook his head. 'Christ, women,' he muttered, and pushed himself away from the building.

With a glance towards the bank, he went towards the hotel. He'd been headed there anyway, but wanted to give the girl enough time to check in before entering himself.

The hotel lobby was furnished with expensive furniture of dark wood, velvet cushions and carved legs with ball and claw feet. A crystal chandelier sparkled with sunlight arcing through huge double windows. Not a speck of dust showed and carpets had been freshly scrubbed. Some sort of perfume hung in the air; he could have done without it.

The young woman had reached the top of the stairway flanking the back wall that led to the upper level. She paused at the top, throwing a glance behind her and spotting him. He tipped his hat. She ignored the gesture, turning away, then striding along the landing until she disappeared into a hallway.

The clerk behind the counter looked up from a register as Hannigan approached.

'Welcome to Revelation Pass, sir,' he said, one of those stupid smiles on his face.

'Skip the speech, I've already heard it.' He reached into a pocket and drew out a roll of greenbacks. Peeling off a number of them, he tossed them onto the polished countertop. He returned the remainder to his pocket. 'Give me a room for the week.'

The clerk stared at him a moment. 'I'm powerful sorry, sir. We're filled up.'

Hannigan's brow knotted. 'You just gave a room to that young lady, I reckon.'

The man shifted feet, eyes averting. 'Why, yes, yes, I did, but it was the last room.'

Hannigan plucked the register from the clerk's hands and glanced over the page. He saw one signature: Miss Hannah Garret. 'This a one-room hotel?'

The man licked his lips. 'No.' His voice shook.

'You got a rule about only allowing women?'

Hannigan saw a strange flash of something in the man's eyes. It might have been fright. 'N-no … I…'

Hannigan grabbed the man by the collar

and hauled him half-over the counter. Nerves frayed, he wasn't in any mood to be run around more than he had been already. 'You best decide real fast what excuse you want to use to keep me out of here, then give me a room anyway.'

'Please, sir, I ... I can't...' The man's cheeks turned crimson and his lips quivered.

'Why the hell not? This is a hotel, aint it?'

'I'm certain the young man was merely mistaken, Mr Hannigan. He would be only too happy to provide you with a room. Isn't that right, Horace?'

Hannigan turned to see the gaunt figure of Pastor Bill standing in back of him. The reverend held the clerk's gaze and the fellow nodded like a jackrabbit. Hannigan released the man, who swept up the money, then deposited a key onto the counter, shaking the whole time. 'R-Room 4...' Sweat streamed down his face now and he looked everywhere but at the pastor and Hannigan.

Hannigan snapped up the key and leaned against the counter, half-turned. 'How the hell you come up on me so quietlike?' He cursed himself for being caught off-guard. It was a mistake manhunters could ill-afford to make.

'You were otherwise occupied, my dear

sir.' Bill spread his hands, a slight smile on his thin lips making him look like a smirking skull.

'All the same...' Hannigan decided the man must have been shadowing him. That only compounded his disgust with himself. 'You got a knack for showing up at just the right moment, don't you?'

'I do the Lord's work, Mr Hannigan. He guides me.'

'Does He really? His work include keeping checks on strangers in town?'

'If need be. Revelation Pass prides itself on filtering out ... certain types.'

'You worried I'm one of those types?'

The man gave him an unreadable expression. 'What type are you exactly, sir? A man of the gun, obviously. Why have you come to this town?'

'Thought I made myself clear earlier. I came looking for a man's daughter. Now I'm lookin' for her killer.'

The pastor studied him and Hannigan got an odd impression from the man. Something about the fellow wasn't quite right. It went beyond the melodramatic preacher act, though Hannigan had met men of the cloth filled full of their own righteousness. He couldn't pinpoint what bothered him, but it brought a prickly feeling to his spine and not many a man could do that to him.

'You will not find your killer in this town, Mr Hannigan. I'm sure whoever committed such a despicable act has long since moved on. It would be best if you followed suit.'

'You don't mind, I think I'll stick around a spell and determine that for myself.'

'It will do you no good.'

'You seem pretty sure of that. You get some kind of divine message on it?' Hannigan made no attempt to conceal his sarcasm.

A shadow crossed Pastor Bill's face, but it came and went so quickly that Hannigan wasn't entirely sure he hadn't imagined it. 'Do not mock the Heavenly Father, Mr Hannigan. His sword is swift and eternal.'

'Like to debate just who's mocking the Almighty, but frankly finding that poor girl's body put me in a downright uncharitable frame of mind. That girl had a future ahead of her and some sonofabitch took it away. She's also got a father who's going to have to live with her loss for the rest of his days. You know what it's like to lose a child, Pastor?'

'I'm afraid I was never so blessed.'

'Strikes me a man of the cloth should understand better than anyone that sin shouldn't go unpunished. A man should never have to bury his children. I aim to see to it he's got a measure of satisfaction that her killer didn't get away with it. You or your town gets in the way of my finding out, expect I won't take it kindly. I make myself clear?'

The pastor nodded. Hannigan thought he caught a sign of some sort of struggle going on behind the man's eyes, but when the preacher spoke the words came calm, almost monotone. 'Tread carefully, Mr Hannigan. The Lord's will be done.'

Fighting a burst of agitation, Hannigan forced a smile, no warmth or humor in the expression. He had little use for men who hid behind lofty standards that they side-stepped at will themselves. He wagered Bill would fit that mold. 'That's likely one thing we can agree on, Pastor.'

Hannigan pushed away from the counter and headed for the door. He would retrieve his gear from the livery where he'd boarded his horse. It would give him a chance to cool down a bit before deciding on his next course of action. He was letting the girl's death get to him, letting it become personal. That would not help him find her killer. Already it had caused his focus to wander just long enough for the pastor to come up on him. Had the man been some hardcase, Hannigan wouldn't have gotten a chance to correct the error.

As he opened the hotel door he glimpsed a flutter of blue at the top of the landing. A figure edged back from the wall's edge, disappearing into the hall. Hannigan knew that the pastor, his back to the stairway, hadn't noticed the girl standing there, eavesdropping. A hint of a smile trickled across the manhunter's lips. Perhaps Pastor Bill wasn't the only one who had angels on his side, but until Hannigan found the girl's killer, he needed to rein in his emotions, make certain he made no more slips.

CHAPTER FOUR

Hannah Garret hurried back to her hotel and eased the door shut. A frown creased her lips as she leaned against the jamb. Something was wrong. That pastor had slipped up behind Hannigan too easily. The manhunter had looked distracted, more so than she had seen him since knowing him over the past two months. But why? This was supposed to be just a simple locate and return mission, nothing dangerous, though after meeting a few of the townsfolk she wondered if something unusual weren't going on. After all, who the devil made strangers register upon arrival?

That newspaper job-opening in the *Standard* window was a piece of luck. She'd planned to set herself up somewhere temporarily, just long enough to establish Amy Breck's whereabouts. Dragging the girl back to Wolf's Bend against her will wasn't something she'd been looking forward to, but the girl was too young to be running off on her own and it had to be done. Her father had her best interests at heart, and Amy would have to realize that.

The way you would have at that age?

She smiled. She reckoned not. She had been a pretty wild spirit then; many would say she still was. But Amy didn't need to leave a father who loved her. She was lucky in that way. Another girl, long ago, never got that choice. Hannah planned to use that very argument on Amy Breck once they located the girl.

Hannah. She still found the name difficult to get used to. It belonged to her grandmother, a woman she'd never known. All

73

she had were a few personal notes penned in elegant handwriting, written to her parents shortly after their daughter was born. Her grandmother died shortly after that, and not six years later...

She swallowed hard at the emotion rising in her throat. She hadn't known her parents, or at least she remembered precious little about them, having been only six years old when they died at the hands of bandits. She'd watched them die, but that memory only came to her in nightmares. In the daylight she blocked it from her mind, afraid to let it rise and fracture the strength she'd fought so hard to build.

She'd been sent to live with her aunt and uncle, but even at that age she'd nursed a bitter hatred for those who preyed on others, so much hatred she had proved too much of a handful. Given to fits of rage, uncontrollable weeping and frequent night terrors, she'd been shipped to a home, where she remained until she ran off at sixteen, hell-bent on somehow finding whoever was responsible for her folks' murders.

But those bandits were long gone, the notion a will-o'-the-wisp. The best she could do was try to help others who had suffered a loss, like herself. It gave her a focus, a calling, had hardened her. For years, that mission was all that mattered to her – until a man named Jim Hannigan came along and showed her she still had some feelings left.

She didn't want to lose him, the way she had lost others. Perhaps that was what had made her decide to double back from her room and watch him from the landing. Or perhaps it was the flicker of something on his face when she passed him on the street, the hard glint in his eye when he spotted the bank-man. Something was wrong, though at this point she didn't know whether it involved their mission here. At that instant it had occurred to her it would be best if she and Jim weren't seen as friendly. So she had slapped him and pranced off like a fancy showhorse. She reckoned she'd catch hell for that later.

She pushed herself away from the jamb and dragged her portmanteau to the bed. Surveying the room, she noted the plump mattress with crisp sheets. Blue wallpaper ornamented with gold *fleurs-de-lis* appeared fresh. A dark wood bureau held a porcelain basin and pitcher.

She went to the window and whisked aside the lace panels, then gazed out into the afternoon street. Folks still milled about as though they were in a daze, smiling. She shook her head.

Did that scrawny preacher fella she had watched come up behind Hannigan have anything to do with the town's strange manner? She had studied him carefully as he came into the hotel so quietlike, all the while her hand on the derringer in her pocket. She reckoned a man of the cloth wasn't particularly threatening but something in his manner put her on the alert. She noted no love lost between him and Hannigan during their brief conversation, too. Had Jim met the man already? Or did he know him from somewhere in the past?

She reckoned Hannigan had come in contact with a lot of people before meeting her; there was much about his past she didn't know. Despite her curious questions over the past two months, many of which he readily answered, he always seemed to hold something back, lock away part of himself. While she felt certain their feelings for each other had grown considerably since meeting in Castigo Pass, she wondered if he'd ever trust her completely.

'I've got your back, Hannigan...' she whispered, wrapping her arms about herself and frowning.

Maybe it wasn't entirely fair to ask him to share everything at this point, especially since she held her own secrets so close to her vest. Neither was used to looking out for anyone but themselves. Trust took time.

She turned from the window, sighing, then went to the bed. Hoisting the portmanteau onto the mattress, she opened the compartments and pulled out a purple sateen bodice. She laid it on the bed, staring at the garment. So much for modesty, but it was a disguise she had used effectively a couple months back and it might serve her well again. A spectre of doubt crept into her mind at the thought of how puritanical Revelation Pass appeared. What if they didn't allow any whores? She recollected seeing a saloon, but it had been closed. Was that only during the day? She hoped so. She also hoped they'd find no sign of Amy Breck working there. That was something she had no desire to report to the gal's father, but too many times girls wound up drawn into that seedy world of fast money and loathsome opportunity.

'No use frettin' over it till you know for sure,' she muttered, pulling a whalebone corset, frilly skirt and high-laced boots from the suitcase, then tossing them onto the bed.

Flipping open a flap in the portmanteau's

left compartment, she revealed an oval mirror. She stared at her reflection, mahogany eyes narrowing. She really didn't look natural as a blonde, did she? Not with her Mexicali complexion and dark eyes.

With a small laugh she plucked the 'Rubens' hat from her head and tossed it into the suitcase. Next, she tugged at more pins embedded into her hair at either side, dropping them into the case as she pried them loose. A moment later she lifted the blonde wig from her head and stowed it in the case. She undid a mesh cap that pressed her own hair tightly against her skull, deposited it atop the wig, then fluffed her ebony locks, which fell just below her shoulders. Running her fingers through her hair, she decided to keep it straight this time instead of curling it into tight ringlets, way she had the last time she'd posed as a woman of the line.

Within the portmanteau she located a leather-covered case and unhooked the latch. The case held numerous tins of make-up and powders, as well as horsehair extensions and false eyelashes. She selected a tin of coral and daubed her cheeks, then applied kohl above her eyes and smeared too-red lipstick across her full lips, changing the contours and flavor of her face nearly completely from that of a prim Southern belle to a wild and woolly woman of the night.

'Tootie, you're a catch,' she muttered, satisfied with the transformation.

She plucked the derringer from her pocket, set it on the bed. She slipped out of the coat and dress, rolled them into a bundle then stuffed them into the portmanteau. She unlaced her fancy polished shoes and kicked them under the bed. Stripping off her chemise, she frowned at the thought of the corset. After what seemed an eternity and countless groans mixed with curses, she managed to stuff herself into the torture-device, wondering if she'd been eating a bit too well on the trail. By the time she had her modest bosom plumped into the purple bodice, she promised herself that on their next case she was going to disguise herself as a nun. After slipping on a skirt and making a last check in the mirror, she closed the case, burying Hannah Garret for the night and setting Tootie del Pelado loose on Revelation Pass. As she dropped the derringer between her breasts, she reckoned the town was never going to know what hit it.

Jacob Quimby stared at the whiskey bottle on the table in the room above the general store. Beside the bottle lay a Bowie knife. He'd closed the shop early, too shaken to continue business after that fella rode in with that poor girl's body. Things were starting to go to hell, exactly the way he'd warned Hanely and Hallet they would. He didn't know exactly who that Hannigan fella was, but he bet it was short step from him to some sort of retribution for the sins they had committed over the past twenty months. Christamighty, he'd told them that pastor was getting more loco by the day. Hanging that girl out there for all to see...

At least that girl was stranger. She'd only been in town a short time and choosing her name in the lottery meant one of their own would not be sacrificed to that monster hiding behind the cloth.

Monster. Was Bill any worse than the three of them? Was he really? They drew the names and brought the girls to their doom, all in a selfish effort to save their pitiful little lives and a town that was some sort of fairy-tale book place during the day and poison at night.

'That dead girl was someone's daughter,' he whispered. He grabbed the whiskey bottle and downed a huge gulp, tears flooding his eyes. And last night...

He choked down another swallow, a pitiful sound escaping his lips and whiskey dribbling from his lips. Last night it had been his Alyssa's turn, way he knew it would be one day if he didn't get her married off to some fella. She hadn't wanted any of the men in this town, had some foolish dreams of working for a big paper in Denver.

He slammed a fist against the table and tears slipped down his face. 'Damn her,' he whispered. 'Damn her. Why couldn't she just listen to me? Why couldn't she have just settled down with some nice young fella and raised family?'

He wanted to hate her for refusing to listen, but couldn't. It wasn't her fault. It was theirs, the three of them. And Bill. But mostly it was his own, because he had been too damn weak to resist them. He had given up his first and only born to save himself. Christ, if his wife had been alive to witness what a pitiful waste he had become ... she would have never forgiven him for what he did. Never. And rightly so. He could never forgive himself. He'd made a horrible mistake, one that would haunt him for the rest of his life.

Hanely and Hallet, they were stronger than he, had no family. Hanely was a bachelor, always had been, far as Quimby knew. The banker had a spark of decency, but was governed by the needs of the many. Easy for him; he didn't have to sacrifice one of his own. He merely took from others.

And Hallet, Hallet had his wife. Rumor had it he had never touched her, only whores. Hallet was weak, but in a different way from Quimby. Quimby sincerely believed Hallet took some sort of perverse enjoyment from the lottery. It excited him, bringing those girls to Bill, in a way Quimby didn't understand. The man enjoyed seeing the fear on the faces of those young women.

Christ, if he had half the balls he wished he had, he'd march right over there and shoot Hallet right between the eyes.

'Alyssa...' he whispered, more tears wandering down his face. His gaze rose to the lone window in the room, seeing the day trickling into dusk, knowing that as soon as the sun set the revelry would start.

His gaze shifted to the Bowie on the table. Staring at it for endless moments, he drew slow breaths and struggled to steel himself against the fear threatening to overpower his decision.

He'd always been weak. Too damn weak. But last night ... last night he'd reached bottom. Now it was time for once in his life to be strong.

He gulped a deep drink of the whiskey, then set the bottle down hard on the table. He wiped a forearm across his lips.

'Forgive me, Alyssa. Please ... I'm so goddamned sorry...'

He grabbed the knife and thrust its edge against his left wrist, drawing a trickle of blood and a sharp bite of pain. Fingers white, his hand started to quake and sweat zigzagged down his face. His eyelids fluttered and his breath stuttered.

Please, give me the strength ... just this once ... please let me die.

Seconds dragged by. He could hear his heart thud and the roar of his blood in his veins. His daughter's face rose before his mind's eye.

Oh, God, I can't, I can't...

He pulled the knife from his wrist, a rush of fury careening through him at his lack of will. He hurled the knife. It ricocheted from a wall across the room, skidded to a stop beneath the table. Cradling his face in his hands, he sobbed violently.

The room darkened about him and a draught brushed his hands. He withdrew his face from his hands, bleary-eyed, struggling to focus through the tears and liquor. A shadow seemed to swell from the gloom beside the table.

'What the hell are you doing here?' he blurted, fear jumping into his belly.

The man smiled, gaunt face demonic in the dusky light. 'Why, Brother Quimby, you are in pain. I have come to ease your worries.'

'Get the hell out of here, you bastard!' His words came out with far less force than he would have liked, but he still felt intimidated by the sonofabitch. The man dressed in the cloth, but Quimby knew him for what he truly was – a sadistic hardcase with a mercurial personality who could flip from wooden benevolence to black rage with the tick of the second-hand. 'I may have to deal with you once a month for your goddamned lottery but I'll be damned if you can just walk into my place of business whenever you take the notion.'

Pastor Bill forced a smile. The expression brought a chill to Quimby and a passing thought asked him if he were strong enough to grab the knife under the table, thrust it between the man's ribs and end the town's imprisonment. But there were others, Bill's deacons, as he called them. How many exactly, none of them knew. Enough to destroy this town, that was for certain.

'I go wherever I like, Brother Quimby.' Bill's voice lost most of it falseness now. The tone was harsh, that of a man used to giving orders and getting exactly what he wanted. 'You should know that by now.' The man smiled again and his voice settled back into an ingratiating monotone. 'But I have come here to ease your suffering, and assure you your Lord cares about your pain.'

Quimby's lips trembled. 'You killed my daughter.'

Bill's hand touched the table edge, finger running along it while his colorless eyes glittered in the dusk. The other hand slipped into his coat pocket. 'Why, I did no such thing. Your daughter is quite among the living.'

Somehow the words gave Quimby a burst of hope, though he damn well knew better than to believe a man like Pastor Bill. 'You killed that poor Breck girl...'

Bill gave a slight nod. 'She was ... impure. You know that is unacceptable.'

'We didn't know. You could have just let her go. Now someone else knows.'

'Mr Hannigan will have his killer soon enough.'

Quimby eyed the man. 'What the hell do you mean?'

85

Bill's smile widened. 'That is none of your concern, Brother Quimby.'

'Where the hell's my daughter, you bastard? I want her back if she's still alive. We'll give you someone else.'

'That is quite impossible, I assure you. She's going to a better place...'

Quimby came half-out of his chair, unable to stand completely as the whiskey made his head spin and his legs rubbery. 'You did kill her, you lousy–'

Bill's hand came up, shoving the older man back into his seat. 'Brother Quimby, I find your language and tone quite distressing. You know the rules just as well as the others.'

'I know 'em, but goddamned if I'll be held forever by the likes of you.'

'Oh, I think you will. You gave me your daughter after all.'

Quimby stared up at the man, cursing himself for shaking and for knowing the sonofabitch was right. He was too weak to fight him, too weak to put a knife into him, and too weak to save his own soul from the fires of hell.

'I saw you waver today.' Bill placed a hand on the man's shoulder; Quimby had the urge to recoil, as if a black widow had crawled up his arm. 'Mr Hannigan will be around to talk to all of you, you realize that, don't you?'

Quimby nodded. 'I know it.'

'The other two, I can trust them not to break down, at least at this point. I cannot trust you, Brother Quimby. Your pain is too great. I realized that earlier. I thought last night that you might realize your sacrifice was for the good of everyone in this town, but today on the street ... well, Brother Quimby, the Lord spoke to me. He told me how your guilt would eat at you. Guilt is the Devil's handmaiden, Brother Quimby. Every hour of every day you'll see your daughter's face. Satan will tempt you with that until you tell Mr Hannigan enough to ruin all we have worked so hard to accomplish in this town. Mr Hannigan would not understand that we do the Lord's work here.'

Quimby wanted to brush the man's hand from his shoulder but couldn't even muster the strength to do that. 'I ... won't tell him anything...' The words came mumbled, a lie written on them, and Bill just smiled the spider smile.

'No, Brother Quimby, you will not. As a man of the Word, I would be remiss if I didn't do all within my power to drive the Devil from your heart.'

Quimby's gaze lifted to the man's face. Through blurred vision he saw a sudden vile light flooding the pastor's colorless gaze. 'You–'

The pastor's free hand came from his pocket, clutching a derringer.

Quimby tried to stand again, knocking over the whiskey bottle. Pastor Bill, hand still on Quimby's shoulder, forced the shopkeeper back into his chair. Amber liquid washed across the table and dripped into Quimby's lap.

'You were distraught, Brother Quimby. You were seeing poor Miss Breck and paying for her favors. She decided to blackmail you, threatened tell your daughter about the entire thing. So you decided to do something about it, silence her forever.'

'No ... no...' Quimby shook his head, panic rushing into his mind.

'Yes, Mr Quimby. You see, you couldn't face the guilt you felt over young Miss Breck's murder, so you closed your shop early. Everyone in town saw the sign in the window. You came up here to free yourself from the prison of your shame, to exorcise the demons clutching at your soul.' Bill's hand suddenly withdrew from Quimby's shoulder. The pastor clamped his forearm around Quimby's neck, jamming it hard against the shopkeep's Adam's apple. Quimby's head jerked back. His mouth came open as he choked.

Bill shoved the derringer into Quimby's mouth and pulled the trigger. Twice.

CHAPTER FIVE

With the sound of a gunshot Jim Hannigan went to his hotel window and peered out into the encroaching night. A man charged down the wide main street on a big bay, blasting away with a Colt into the air and whooping at the top of his lungs.

'What the hell?' Hannigan muttered. Surprise pinched his features. Had anyone told him some cowboy would be hurrahing this town after what he'd witnessed upon his arrival he would have laughed. He blinked, wondering if he hadn't been on the trail too long.

The cowboy blasted off three more shots and careened past with a yell that threatened to snap his vocal cords.

The hurrahing worked like a clanging

dinner-bell, signaling a revelry the likes of which Hannigan had seen in few towns. God knew he'd been in some hellholes but what occurred in the street below would have given the most lawless town competition.

Folks flooded into the streets like cattle out of a chute. Cowboys with whiskey bottles clutched in their grips, painted women with wanton smiles. A few gals wore only their undergarments; they were quickly thrust against walls by randy cowhands who pawed their bodies and committed acts in public that shocked even Hannigan.

A horde of men charged towards the saloon and, as the window was half-raised, he suddenly heard the clanking of a piano ring out, followed by waves of raucous laughter and whoops. Another gunshot thundered from somewhere. Two men crashed through a rail and did their damnedest to pound each other into oblivion.

He backed away from the window, brow scrunched. He grabbed his Stetson from the bedpost, set it on his head and stood in the darkened room. He'd been figuring on pumping the saloonkeeper for information, having spotted the drinkerie on his walk through town earlier that day and now seemed as good a time as any. It would give him a chance to survey the rowdiness first hand.

The town and its occupants had perplexed him with their blissful composure, but that was nothing to the puzzlement he felt now. He had pondered how a young woman like Amy Breck wound up dead in such a peaceful town, but maybe it was no longer such a mystery. The only questions were who and what caused this town to react at opposite extremes, and what had the Breck girl gotten snared in that resulted in her death?

He went to the door, stepped out into the hallway and glanced about for any sign of Tootie, but her door was closed. The clerk had given him a room a few doors down.

After locking the door he went to the lobby, then strolled out into the night, finding a body lying on the boardwalk in front of the door. The man was bloodied and groaning, the victim of a brawl, but a glance told Jim the fellow would recover soon enough. He stepped over him and headed towards the saloon.

'Hey, gent, buck for a buck, if you know what I mean...' The girl was leaning against the side of a building, her hard features caked with warpaint, eyes glazed. She slipped down a corner of her peek-a-boo blouse, exposing her left breast. Her trembling hand drifted across her ample bounty and her tongue slipped over lips blood-red with too much lipstick.

He ignored her and she muttered something unintelligible but obviously vulgar, then spat at his back.

He turned, anger and disgust hardening his face. She looked at him with an odd expression, something that inspired pity instead of anger, and he realized she was no more than sixteen. 'Go home, child,' he said.

She shook her dirty-blond head. 'Home ain't safe, not in this town. Better on the street, mister.' A spectre of fear peered through the daze in her eyes.

'What the hell made this town the way it is? What are you afraid of?'

The girl tugged up her blouse and a look of panic snapped the dullness completely from her gaze. 'Nothing, mister. Nothing at all.'

'I can protect you, child, if you tell me.'

'No, you can't. No one can.' She pushed herself away from the wall, spun, then ran off, high-laced shoes clomping on the boards. Hannigan watched her go, pity welling, along with a sense of defeat. Sometimes it seemed not to matter how many he helped, because another would always slip away.

A man brushed by Hannigan, jostling him hard. The manhunter flung the fellow from him, frustration getting the better of him.

The cowboy slammed against the wall and looked up, half-stunned, half-drunk. He chuckled, drool slithering from his mouth. 'Sorry, fella...' Laughing harder, the man staggered away.

'Christ...' Hannigan muttered. Ahead of him another girl squatted on the boardwalk, relieving herself, while her cowboy companion roared with laughter, then booted her over into the puddle of her own urine. The girl giggled and made a clumsy effort to get to her feet and haul up her undergarments.

Hannigan fought the disgust making his gut churn and stepped off the boardwalk to avoid the couple.

Reaching the saloon a moment later, he wondered what he'd find once he entered. If what he'd seen so far were any indication, it wouldn't be pretty. He paused before the batwings, a twinge of worry over Tootie rising in his mind.

She's more than capable of taking care of herself, Hannigan.

That's what he kept telling himself. But lately he found it impossible not to fret over her safety. The thought that their line of work was just too damned dangerous and every case risked her life had played on his mind more and more over the past two months. That was why he had picked this case, because it supposedly posed little jeopardy.

You know how to stop those feelings, don't you?

He did, but the thought of it was nearly as frightening as losing her on a mission.

Shaking from his thoughts, he pushed through the batwings and stepped into hell.

The newspaper had closed shop for the night when Bertrim Hanely entered, shutting the door behind him. A lantern burned on a table next to rolled-out newsprint, which John Hallet leaned over, checking type with a jeweler's loop. Hallet gazed up, nodded to Hanely, who gave an acknowledging lift of his chin.

'The note said we were to meet here instead of Quimby's shop.' Hanely said it, half as question, wondering why the hell the location had suddenly changed after all these months.

Hallet straightened and tossed the loop onto the table. 'Struck me as odd, too.'

Hanely glanced about the office. 'Where the hell is Quimby? He's usually first in.'

Hallet shrugged. 'Damned if I know. I figured it was him when I heard the door open, but I haven't seen hide of him since earlier today.'

Hanely didn't like the sensation that slithered down his back. And he didn't like a third meeting in as many days. He didn't like the fact that some manhunter had ridden in looking for the Breck girl and even less that the man had come across her hanging from a tree outside of town.

Hanely cleared his throat, fighting the nervous flutter in his belly. 'Things are getting out of hand. Quimby was right. That was a goddamn bad idea leaving that body out there for all to see.'

'Tsk-tsk, Brother Hanely,' came a voice from the back. 'Question not the Lord's judgment. It puts the soul at risk.' The gaunt pastor stepped from the shadows at the back, his face frozen with the beatific expression Hanely had come to loathe.

'Dammit, Bill, bad enough you force us to do your bidding, but that stage-preacher act really sets my nerves on edge.' Hanely said it before he could stop himself, finding his anger and guilt over sending Quimby's daughter to some unknown doom had eaten away a measure of his composure. It was one thing delivering strangers to that madman, but another doing it to one of their own.

Pastor Bill's expression didn't change but something vicious crossed his eyes. 'The fires of Hell consume thy willful words, Brother Hanely. See that they do not rise up high enough to devour you.'

Hanely repressed the urge to shudder. The man actually sounded half-serious with his idiotic talk. He was goddamn loco, just the way Quimby said.

'How'd you get in here?' asked Hallet. 'Thought I locked the back way.'

Bill's colorless gaze fell on Hallet and the mousy man clamped his mouth shut. Hanely knew the little weasel was intimidated by Bill, though it could be rightly said they all were. 'The Lord provides, Brother Hallet. The Lord provides.'

Hanely winced, every word from the man scraping up one side of his nerves and down the other. 'We're waiting on Quimby. You haven't seen him, have you?'

Bill drew a long breath, his chest appearing to expand to double its size, then sink back, as the breath wheezed back out. The man wasn't large but something about the way his body almost uncoiled hinted at a strength few would have expected.

'Ah, poor Brother Quimby. He was overly distraught at the thought of sacrificing his daughter, did you know that?'

Hanely nodded. 'Any fool could see that. Where is he? Why isn't he here yet?' Hanely didn't like the notion clawing its way into his mind.

Bill strolled forward, running a finger along the long table, causing Hallet to back away a couple steps. 'I'm afraid he won't be joining us tonight, Brother Hanely. That's why I called this meeting. You see, the poor man proved much weaker in spirit than the two of you. Much weaker. In fact, he couldn't abide with what he had done.'

'What the devil do you mean?' Hanely's gut plunged, a dark suspicion running through his mind.

'Brother Quimby was distraught over something else, did you know that? A terrible secret, in fact, involving young Amy Breck.'

'Amy Breck?' Hallet's brow crinkled. 'He didn't even know her till the night we brought her to you.'

'Oh, but he did, Brother Hallet. He admits it right here in his suicide note.' Bill fished in a pocket of his dark suit and brought out a bloodstained note. He passed it towards Hallet but Hanely stepped forward, snatching the paper, the sick feeling in his belly exploding into full nausea.

'Suicide note?' Hallet shook his head. 'Quimby was upset but he wouldn't...' He stopped, catching Bill's colorless gaze. He seemed to deflate and leaned against the table.

Hanely's eyes drifted over the handwriting on the letter, his worst fears confirmed. He knew Quimby's writing, had made the man enough loans at the bank and seen his signature countless times. The handwriting didn't belong to Quimby. It was too drifting, almost scrawl in places. The mark of a disturbed man for certain, but not of Jacob Quimby.

'This can't be...' he muttered, knowing damn well Quimby had not committed suicide. The sonofabitch had murdered him.

Bill gave a reassuring nod. 'I assure you it is. In fact, I just came from Brother Quimby's store. The poor man blew his brains out with a derringer. He's upstairs in his shop right this moment. Flies are having a feast, I would imagine.'

Hanely looked up from the note. 'You sick sonofa—'

'Ah, careful, Brother Hanely. Suicide can be quite catching, I hear. The Devil's tool,

98

the Devil's tool.' The threat in the pastor's voice came plain but greased with that damned hypnotic tone the man used in his sermons. Hanely shut his mouth. When it came down to it, he was likely no stronger than Quimby and just as afraid of Pastor William McKee.

'Why?' asked Hallet, voice shaking. Hanely wagered the man was more afeared over his own mortality than upset over Quimby's death.

'Read the note, Brother Hallet. Quimby murdered that poor Breck girl and his guilt drove him to make amends to his God. Little did he realize suicide exiles a soul from heaven's gates.'

'You didn't have to do this,' Hanely said. 'He wouldn't have talked. We could have kept him in line.'

Bill smiled the spider smile. 'I did nothing, sir. I am merely the Lord's humble messenger.'

You crazy sonofabitch, Hanely wanted to say, but kept his tongue reined. He had no desire to follow in Quimby's footsteps, no matter how much the notion of the man's death sickened him. 'We finished here?' He prayed they were, but had a suspicion more was coming.

Bill began walking towards the door, silent for a moment. He paused, his back to them, head lifting. 'There is one small thing...' He turned. 'Deliver that note to Mr Hannigan. Inform him his case is solved and there's no need for him to look further for Amy Breck's killer. He has his man.'

Hanely didn't think his belly could have dropped any further but he swore it did now. 'Hannigan won't believe that.'

'But of course he will. He can't deny the evidence right in your hand, Brother Hanely. You can find Mr Hannigan at the saloon, I imagine. One of my men spotted him headed that way just a short time ago. Make sure he's out of town by tomorrow.'

'What if he won't go?' Hanely had little confidence that Hannigan would take the note at face value. Something in the man-hunter's eyes had told Hanely there was a man of character, one who didn't back down or back off.

'Ah, Brother Hanely, that would be just too bad, wouldn't it?' Bill glanced back at the banker, colorless eyes glittering. Hanely's legs went weak.

Hallet glanced at Hanely, apparently having no taste for the job, either, but he wouldn't dare argue with the preacher.

'Brother Hallet...' Bill's gaze shifted. 'I believe I saw a new young lady in town today. A blonde. She came to your office, did she not?'

Hallet nodded. 'Hannah Garret. She asked for Alyssa Quimby's old job. I gave it to her.'

'Very good, Brother Hallet. I do hope her name will be included in the next drawing. She intrigues me. I may even consider a separate drawing in this case, one for my own...' His smile widened '...comfort...'

Hanely flinched and Hallet nodded like a puppy eager to please its master.

Bill uttered a laugh that sent a shiver down Hanely's back, then stepped out into the night.

Boisterous cowboys and women of the line displaying their wares packed the saloon. Their faces smeared with war paint that couldn't disguise their hollow eyes and saddle-weary expressions, they leaned over shoulders and pressed their flesh into men's faces, while the fellows played poker and gulped whiskey. The piano player banged away at the keys of a tinkler. Old booze, cloying perfume and sweat assailed his nostrils. A cloud of Durham smoke hung in the air.

He spotted fully half a dozen men who

appeared to be hardcases. The type had been absent during the day.

Descending the three steps into the saloon proper, he doffed his Stetson, eyes narrowing. Giving the doves the once over, he spotted a dark-haired woman at the bar, discussing something with the 'keep. She moved away, a hint of a smile on her lips; he reckoned Tootie had infiltrated the saloon. The thought stabbed him with a spike of jealousy he couldn't deny. She avoided looking in his direction, though he wagered she knew he was here. She had a way of seeing everything and she was capable of things he still wondered about.

He threaded his way through the jammed tables towards the bar.

'Hey there, honeybun, give old Stacey a whirl?' A young woman gripped his arm, her words slurred and her bosom hanging half-out of her blue sateen bodice. He jerked his arm free and she cast him an annoyed expression, then stumbled off towards better prospects.

Reaching the bar that ran along the west wall, he pulled out a stool and settled onto it, tossing his hat onto the next stool. 'Whiskey,' he said, as the 'keep came up to him. The man was a bag of bones, carried a haunted expression in his eyes. He reached to a hutch behind him and withdrew a bottle. He set it before Hannigan.

'Just a glass.' Hannigan reached into his pocket and drew out a roll of greenbacks.

'Only sell it by the bottle,' the man said.

Hannigan raised an eyebrow. 'The hell?'

'You heard me. Buy the bottle or get the hell out.' Hannigan resisted the urge to throttle the man. It wouldn't help him get any information at this point. 'How much?'

'Twenty dollars.'

'Judas Priest!' Hannigan's voice raised. 'I could get a whore cheaper than that.'

The 'keep uttered a sharp laugh. 'Twenty dollars or–'

'Get the hell out, I know.' Hannigan peeled off the bills, more than a bit irritated. But with the prices he charged his clients, he reckoned he couldn't bitch too much. He returned the remainder of his roll to his pocket, then uncapped the bottle and took a swig. The whiskey tasted like cat-piss.

'That dark-haired gal you were just talkin' to...' He set the bottle back on the counter.

'Tootie, her name is. She's new here. Right pretty. You lookin' to take a tumble with her?'

'Might give her a turn. She's a looker, that's for damn sure.'

'Cost ya plenty. Best-lookin' whore in the place.'

'Most sober, too.'

The 'keep raised an eyebrow. 'You come in here to criticize the whores?'

Hannigan uttered a small laugh. 'Reckon not. Fact, I'm new to your town. Rode in during the day. Bit different here at night, ain't it?'

The 'keep shifted feet, eyeing him, as if wondering if there weren't something more behind the question, then apparently deciding there was not. 'Pastor Bill says we can't know salvation if we don't know sin, that sins of the flesh is fine long as it's contained to certain hours.'

'Pastor Bill. Reckon I met him a time or two today. Seems like a peculiar gent.'

The 'keep's face darkened. 'Best not to speak ill of the good reverend, fella. He's been a blessing to this town.'

'Has he? Seems to me he's got y'all cinched tighter than a whore's corset during the day.'

'He knows what's best for us.'

Hannigan took another swig of his whiskey, wincing at the taste, then studied the bartender. Something lay behind the man's eyes when he talked of the pastor. That something might have been fear or some kind of perverse compulsion to believe a holy man's word blindly, the way some folks did. He wasn't sure which.

'He didn't know what was best for that poor Breck girl, now, did he?'

Was that a flash of panic in the barman's eyes? 'You ask some mighty odd questions, gent,' he said, a hitch in his voice.

Hannigan decided to slap the cards on the table. 'Her pa sent me after her, to bring her home. I ain't all-fired happy 'bout telling him she's coming back in a box. That gal didn't deserve what happened to her.'

The bartender shrugged. 'Reckon none of 'em do.' He immediately caught himself and the panic jumped back into his eyes.

'None of 'em?' Hannigan's gut cinched. 'Amy Breck not the only girl found dead in this town?'

The bartender shook his head, too fast. 'No, hell, no. She's the only dead girl in this town for years.'

Hannigan's eyes narrowed, held the man's gaze. 'I reckon some folks in this town, yourself included, knew that gal was hangin' out there. Why didn't anybody cut her down?' His voice held an edge that brooked no argument.

The man ran his tongue over chapped lips.

'Wasn't our place.'

'What the hell does that mean?'

'Please, I said more than I should have. I don't know who you are, mister, but don't go askin' questions in this town. I'm sorry that gal's dead, but it ain't our fault. Ain't nothin' we can do about it.'

'I get me the powerful notion a hell of a lot more's going on in this town than folks want to say. Strikes me as damn peculiar your sweet little town turns into Satan's ball the moment dusk hits. Strikes me even stranger a poor girl winds up hanging from a tree and not a damn one of you bothered to cut her down 'fore the buzzards had their fill.'

The barman's face bleached. 'You don't know what can happen if you keep sayin' things like that, fella.'

'Then why don't you tell me before I take a notion to send a federal marshal down here and let him sort you all out?'

The barkeep's eyes widened suddenly and he stepped back.

Hannigan stiffened as he felt a hand land on his shoulder. He turned, slowly, cursing himself for again getting distracted enough not to realize a man – correct that – *two* men had come up behind him.

Both had the looks of hardcases. One

stood to either side of him and he could see in their eyes that they had a lather up and weren't about to be talked out of it. Hannigan caught the stench of whiskey and sweat about both. He also noted from the corner of his eye that Tootie had paused beside a table, her gaze locked on them.

His tone evened. 'You fellas best take it somewhere else. You don't want to push your luck.'

One of the men, a fellow with a blocky face and greased-back black hair, grinned. 'Our gal, Stacey, said you were right unkindly to her, stranger. Ain't that right, Jasper?'

Jasper, a bald man with a scar on his neck, nodded. 'Sounds about right to me, Jenkins. Downright rude, she said. Pretty gal like Stacey and this fella just treats her like she was cowdung.'

Jasper shook his head. 'Ain't right, is it? Ain't right at all.'

Hannigan saw Jenkins's arm twitch, then jerk up and forward. It was a clumsy blow, telegraphed.

Hannigan exploded from his stool, thrusting himself forward and down as the blow came at him. The swing swooshed over his head and he drove his skull into Jenkins's belly. The hardcase blew out an explosive breath and stumbled backwards.

Hannigan straightened, stepped towards the hardcase, but Jenkins got his balance, launched another roundhouse the manhunter easily avoided. Hannigan snapped a short uppercut. The blow drove Jenkins's head straight up as if it had suddenly come unhinged like a flung-open box-lid. A glaze invaded the man's eyes and he staggered, legs rubbery.

A bottle ricocheted from the side of Hannigan's forehead. He caught its descent from the corner of his eye but couldn't get out of the way completely. Stars exploded before his vision.

He stumbled, almost going down. The room spun before his eyes and he caught a glimpse of Tootie sliding forward, her own hand clamped about the neck of a whiskey bottle.

Jenkins, recovering, lunged at Hannigan. The manhunter pivoted, the move clumsy, off balance, but good enough to swing the hardcase over a hip and send him flying into a table. The table collapsed and the hardcase hit the floor atop it, a cloud of sawdust billowing up.

Jasper dove forward again, bottle upraised. Hannigan would have been brained this time, but Tootie stuck out a foot as the man lunged.

The hardcase pitched forward and slammed face first into the floor. The whiskey bottle flew from his grip. His head lifted, blood bubbling from his lips but little damaged otherwise.

Hannigan, vision now focused but his head pounding, took two steps towards Jasper and kicked him full force in the teeth. The blow might have killed the man had he not been partially drunk and tough as old horse steak. As it was, a number of his teeth sprinkled the floor and he curled into a ball, groaning.

Arms fastened around Hannigan's waist and he tried to twist. Jenkins had recovered faster than the manhunter expected and gotten to his feet. He hoisted Hannigan off the floor and hurled him sideways. The hardcase had a good deal of strength and momentum on his side. The manhunter slammed into a table and rebounded, hitting the floor on a shoulder.

Fury exploded within him at his poor performance in the fight, but he still felt old injuries plaguing him from the last case; two months had not been enough to recover completely. He rolled onto his side, seeing Tootie maneuvering behind the man.

He didn't want her cover blown, so he gritted his teeth and pushed himself up, coming to his feet just as Jenkins swung a hammering blow intended to crack Hannigan's skull. The manhunter thrust a fist deep into the man's groin. The hardcase's punch sailed over Hannigan's shoulder and he let out a pitiful half-screech. He collapsed on top of Hannigan and the manhunter, straightening, hurled him to the floor. Jenkins curled into a ball, blood streaming from his lips, moaning.

Hannigan, legs shaking, stumbled to the bar. The room had gone silent, cowhands and whores alike watching in open-mouthed eagerness. A fever pervaded the room, a barely contained bloodlust. They reminded him of caged animals eager to shed their captors.

He grabbed his Stetson from the stool and jammed it on his head. With gasped breaths, he staggered towards the batwings, no one making a move to stop him. In fact, the revelry picked up exactly where it had left off, folks stepping over the fallen hardcases as if they didn't exist.

As he reached the batwings strength came back into his legs and his nerves steadied. His head would pound for a spell, and his shoulder would likely ache tomorrow, but that was the extent of it.

He glanced back at the barroom, seeing Tootie looking inconspicuous but knew she was watching him from the corner of her eye. One of the hardcases, Jasper, was pulling himself up onto a chair, but showed no inclination to pursue Hannigan for a second round. It occurred to Hannigan that more lay behind the attack than the simple defense of a bargal's honor. Either on their own or by someone's order, they'd elected to send him a clear message: Get out – you don't belong here.

As he pushed through the batwings the sultry night air hit his face.

Two men stood before him on the boardwalk. His hand swept towards the ivory handle of the Peacemaker at his hip.

CHAPTER SIX

'After what just happened in that saloon you're damned lucky I didn't blow either of your heads off.' Hannigan held his ivory-gripped Peacemaker straight-armed at the two men standing on the boardwalk. As its sawed-off bore shifted from one to the other, fear tightened the muscles in each man's jaw and widened his eyes. There never had been any real danger of Hannigan shooting them; the display was more for effect and the soothing of his own annoyance over his performance in the saloon.

'P-Please, Mr Hannigan...' Sweat broke out on Bertrim Hanely's forehead and trickled down his face. 'We had nothing to do with whatever happened in there. Revelation Pass is a rough town at night. Any stranger is best to stick it out in his hotel room, least till he gets acclimated.'

Hallet nodded, rabbitlike, but kept his mouth closed.

Hannigan lowered his gun, then slipped it back into its holster. 'Just what the hell is it with this town, Hanely? During the day it's as saintly as a nun's virtue, then at dusk all hell breaks loose.'

Hanely's eyes averted. 'Please, Mr Hannigan, that's just the way things are here.'

'That ain't no answer, Mr Mayor. Reckon I should ask Pastor Bill?'

Hallet almost smiled. There was something smug about the expression Hannigan damn well didn't like. 'You could certainly ask him, Mr Hannigan.' The mousy man ran a hand through his hair. 'Indeed, you most certainly could.'

Hanely skipped the newspaperman a corrosive glance, but Hallet ignored him.

The manhunter cocked an eyebrow. 'I didn't know better, Mr Hallet, I'd say you're hidin' something about this Bill. Something you're all in favor of me finding out the hard way.'

Hanely cleared his throat. 'Hallet's merely distraught, Mr Hannigan. That's all. He meant nothing by his remark.'

Hannigan's gaze shifted back to Hanely. 'What reason would Mr Hallet have to be distraught, Mr Hanely? Seems you both got this town just the way you like it, 'less you care to tell me what's really up. While you're at it, maybe you'd like to tell me just who your Pastor Bill is and why that girl at the funeral man's is going back to her father in a pine box.' Hannigan's nerves crawled with irritation at the two men in particular and the town in general. Various aching body parts from his saloon fight didn't help matters.

Hanely remained silent for a moment, then reached into his suitcoat and brought out a bloodstained letter. 'Mr Hannigan, you said you wanted that girl's killer, then you would leave. I am presenting you with him, so consider your case solved. I expect you'll be on your way with first light.'

Hannigan let out a small grunt. 'Subtle, Mr Hanely.' He accepted the letter and read the scrawled lines. A neat little package, wasn't it? But was it wrapped in deceit and all tied up with a bow of lies? The note told him Jacob Quimby had murdered the young woman in cold blood and saved the law a trial and trouble of having a gallows built. He'd never seen Quimby's handwriting before, but he reckoned the scrawl on this page sure looked like the work of a man with a saddleful of something burdening his mind.

'Take me to his body.' Hannigan folded the note and stuffed it in a pocket.

Hanely looked at Hallet, then at the manhunter. Neither man spoke.

Hannigan's eyes narrowed. 'Now, Mr Hanely, 'fore I lose my patience.'

Hanely nodded and turned, then stepped off the boardwalk into the street. Hallet followed and Hannigan fell in behind. They led him to the general store, avoiding drunks and sauced-up women along the way. Hanely unlocked the store door and shoved it open.

'After you, Mr Hanely.' Hannigan gave him a grim smile. 'I make it a point never to turn my back on fellas I don't trust.'

Hanely stared at him, as if offended. 'You don't mince words, do you, Mr Hannigan?'

'Not unless I'm with respectable company.'

'Now, see here, you–' A piqued expression tightened Hallet's face.

A challenging smile crossed Hannigan's lips. 'Careful, Mr Hallet. I reckon I wouldn't take very kindly to you tryin' out your backbone at this point.'

Hallet went silent and his face shone crimson even under the poor lighting.

'Just shut the devil up, Hallet,' Hanely said, tone brusque. 'Let's just get this done. It'll be a gruesome job, I imagine.'

'You ain't seen the body yet?' Hannigan questioned. 'This note in my pocket just walk itself to your door?'

A muscle twitched near Hanely's mouth and he seemed to take a moment to gather himself. 'No, no, Mr Hannigan, that's not what I meant. Of course we saw it. It's just that I turned away when we entered the room. Hallet found the note.'

He was lying, and Hannigan's suspicions jumped a few notches. It crossed his mind the two might be leading him into some sort of trap, but he dismissed the notion. Neither appeared to have the *cojones* for that. It was

115

more likely they wanted him to view the body and accept the note as proof the girl's killer had been found, then leave their town.

Hanely and Hallet led Hannigan down an aisle to a rickety wooden staircase at the back. Hallet grabbed a lantern from a countertop and brought it to light, the sulfury smell of his lucifer and the flickering flame making Hannigan feel as if he had just stepped into the anteroom leading to hell.

He followed them up the stairs, casting a backward glance to make certain no one hid in the shadows. Difficult to see anything, so he kept his body wedged sideways as he went up, hand hovering above his Peace-maker, back to the wall.

At the top, the short hall contained only two rooms. Hallet pushed open a door to the one on the left.

Entering the room, Hannigan heard a small sound of horror escape Hanely's lips at the sight of the body doubled over the table. Hallet set the light on the table and turned up the flame. His face appeared bleached, but a strange eagerness glittered in his eyes. Hannigan got the notion there was likely no love lost between the newspaperman and the dead shopkeeper.

The manhunter went to the body. The

dead man's face lay sideways on the table. A pool of blood had soaked into the wood, browning in places. The corpse stared ahead with a sightless gaze that sent a chill skittering down Hannigan's spine. Death was never pretty, but since coming into the town he'd seen it twice in its ugliest form.

He tried to lift the man's torso but stiffness was setting in, telling Hannigan the man had been dead for at least a couple hours.

'When'd you find the body?' the manhunter asked, not looking at the other two.

Hanely shifted feet. 'A-about ... two hours ago, maybe a bit less.'

'Took you that long to get the note to me?' He glanced up at Hanely.

'Couldn't find you at the hotel. We were just about to look in the saloon when you came out.'

The explanation sounded reasonable but something still told Hannigan Hanely was lying.

Hannigan moved the lantern closer to the body. The man's mouth was a gruesome spectacle and an overwhelming urge to pull back gripped him. Black powder coated areas of the gore from the gun's blowback. He glanced at the small weapon gripped in the dead man's right hand. The flesh of that hand was pale and bluish. It would be a spell before he could pry the weapon out without breaking the finger bones, so he wouldn't bother trying. Didn't matter anyway. The derringer was an over-under type, homemade, by its looks, and probably machined with less-than-remarkable precision. He stared at Quimby's hand for a moment, bringing the lantern closer to it.

'You can see he used that gun to kill himself, Mr Hannigan.' Hanely's face welded with a sickened look.

'Gun local made...' Hannigan said, not a question.

Hanely nodded. 'Fella named Frisk here in town. I recognize his work.'

Hannigan's gaze traveled from the dead man's hand to the two men standing near the door, both of whom seemed to be waiting for him to verify the results and announce his departure at the earliest possible moment.

'You are the bank-manager as well as mayor, that right, Hanely?'

Hanely nodded, brow knitting. 'That's right. Mr Hannigan.'

'You ever make this man a loan?'

Hanely tried to hide a glint of worry in his eyes. 'Why, no, Mr Quimby was quite solvent. A very respectable member of the community.'

Hannigan heard a lie in Hanely's voice. 'Then I reckon you wouldn't have a sample of Mr Quimby's handwriting in your files?'

Hanely's spark of worry ignited into a small blaze. 'No, no, I would not. Why ... do you ask?'

'Curiosity, I reckon.' Hannigan would have tried matching a known sample of the shopkeep's handwriting to the note's, but he reckoned he could find some signed paper of some sort in the store if he needed further proof that the man had been murdered. Quimby hadn't killed himself; Hannigan was certain. And in all likelihood the shopkeeper had not murdered Amy Breck, no matter what the note said. Most likely Quimby had not written it.

'Reckon I've seen enough here,' Hannigan said. 'You two best make whatever arrangements for this man you see fit.'

'Then you'll be on your way?' Hallet's voice held more eagerness than he likely intended.

The manhunter started towards the door, a thin smirk turning his lips. 'Why, no, Mr Hallet, I do believe I'll stay in your fine town a spell and partake of some of its hospitality.'

'But you have your killer...' Hanely's voice

119

carried almost a plea.

'Do I, Mr Hanely?' Hannigan held the mayor's gaze. 'Only thing worse than a killer is a stupid one...' He walked from the room. Quimby's corpse had told him all he needed to know about a man's violent death – with the exception of just who had killed him. The murder opened even more questions regarding this town and whatever it was they were hiding.

Hannigan made his way back to his hotel room, realizing that over an hour had slipped away since his fight at the saloon.

When he reached his room he stopped, hand on the handle. He peered behind him along the hallway lit by wall lanterns turned low. He spotted no one.

With one hand he gripped the doorknob while the other fished in a pocket for his key. He halted when the sudden turn of the handle told him the door was already unlocked. A tingle went through his nerves.

He withdrew his hand from his pocket, then eased his Peacemaker from its holster. Bringing the gun up before his chest, he pushed the door inward, standing to the side as it creaked open.

'You gonna stand out there in the hall all night with your gun cocked or you gonna come on in and holster your pistol?' came a woman's voice from within the darkness of his room.

He let out the breath he'd been holding. Slipping his Peacemaker into its holster, he stepped inside and closed the door. A match flared and a lantern came to light on the night-table beside the bed. Tootie blew out the lucifer and smiled up at him from where she sat on the edge of the bed.

'Someday you're gonna have to tell me how you manage to get into locked rooms so easy.'

Her smile widened. 'A gal's gotta have some secrets, doesn't she?'

He doffed his hat and tossed it on the bedpost. 'You didn't have to slap me earlier.'

An innocent look came over her face. 'I saw the expression in your eyes when that man came out of the bank. Besides, you kinda liked it, didn't you?' She winked, mischief dancing in her eyes.

'Funny girl, you are.'

She worked a pout. 'I was trying for seductive.'

'That comes naturally.'

'Why, Mr Hannigan, a compliment?'

Hannigan chuckled, lighting another lantern on the bureau. He poured water from the pitcher into the basin, then splashed it into his face. Toweling off on his shirt-sleeve, he turned to Tootie, who still wore the blue sateen bodice and frilly skirt. 'Anything?'

'No. Just got myself established there, so didn't want to press right away.'

'Can't say I'm all-fired comfortable with you workin' that place, especially after seeing what goes on in this town after nightfall.'

'Why, Mr Jim Hannigan, if I didn't know you better I'd say you had a streak of green running down your hide.'

He hoped the rush of heat into his face didn't show. Damn right he was jealous. What fella wouldn't be with a gal as beautiful as Tootie del Pelado? Damned if he'd give her the satisfaction of knowing it, though.

'Hell, no, just worried over your safety, is all.' His tone didn't sound convincing even to himself.

She raised an eyebrow. 'You could marry me and settle down somewhere...'

She said it jokingly, but enough seriousness came in her tone to send a wave of darkness washing over him. For a moment a distant memory struggled to push into his mind, but he forced it back. 'Maybe we best set you up as a schoolmarm on our next case.'

She frowned, a glint of hurt in her mahogany eyes. 'That ain't no fun at all...' she said, but her heart wasn't in it. 'You find any leads to Amy Breck?'

He nodded, lips tight. He sighed, going to the window and gazing out into the rowdy street. Shouts and whoops, giggles and atonal music came from the night. He closed the window, though the room was overly warm. 'I found *her*.'

Tootie stood, surprise washing over her face. 'What? Where is she?'

He turned back to her. 'She's at the funeral-man's.' He explained his entrance into Revelation Pass and finding her body, as well as the three men he'd encountered and Pastor Bill. He ended by drawing the note from his pocket and handing it to her.

She took it and read it next to the lantern on the nightstand. 'Then the case is over? We have the killer?'

Hannigan shook his head. 'Not by a long shot, I reckon.'

'But this note–'

'Was likely written by someone else. Maybe one of the two remaining men or that Pastor Bill.'

Her brow scrunched. 'This Pastor Bill, he's the one who came up on you in the lobby?'

'That's him. All skinny and morbid and as saintly as a politician. He's got some sort of agenda, I reckon. Maybe this whole town does.'

Concern softened her features. 'Ain't like you to let someone come up on your back, Hannigan. It worries me. Happened again in the saloon.'

He shrugged. 'I reckon it's just that girl ... didn't expect to send her back to her pa that way. She was young, too young. Stupid of her being so headstrong and goin' off on her own that way. Got her fool ass killed.'

She looked at him with a peculiar expression, one that came from somewhere deep within her and asked him to share more. Damn, but he hated that look. It frightened him, and not much frightened a man like Jim Hannigan, a man with a calloused soul.

'Ain't her fault, Hannigan, and you know it. The men we track down, it's their fault. We can't save everyone but we can make sure whoever did this doesn't get the chance to do it again.'

'All the same, maybe it's best you sit this one out. I got a bad feeling about this town.'

'I got the same feeling. Peculiar place by any standards. But I didn't sign up with you to sit in a hotel room waiting to hear you got yourself shot in the back.'

'Tootie...' His voice held a frustrated note.

She giggled. 'Maybe you'd prefer a gal who sits home knitting sweaters?'

'Could use a sweater yourself, dressed like that,' he said before he could stop himself. Fact was, her get-up made all his bells ring, but he didn't need other men getting such notions.

'In this heat? Why, suh, I do declare, I was thinking of shedding all my clothes and running naked through the streets until you caught me...'

'That's the worst Southern belle accent I've ever heard.' He hoped he could change the subject before she brought up any thoughts of marriage again.

'Says you. I practiced it for hours. You're just avoiding the subject again.' She held his gaze, the indictment clear in her eyes. She'd gotten to know him too well in the short time they'd been together. In a way it was comforting, the way they almost functioned as one. In another, it was damned annoying.

'Reckon I owe you a thanks for watching my back in the saloon.'

'And earlier when that preacher fella snuck up on ya, but who's counting?' She winked. Her tone turned serious and the levity faded from her face. 'You know you don't owe me any thanks. If you'd have been in any danger of losing to them I would have stopped them ... *dead*.'

He nodded. 'Reckon I'd best keep my eyes open a bit better.'

She searched his face for something he didn't want to reveal to her. She knew it anyway, he figured. No point in bringing it into the open.

'You could just say it, Jim...' Her voice came low, as if not really expecting any answer.

But he couldn't say it, because it meant admitting that his distraction came from feelings he never thought he would have for a woman. It would change things, rope him into something he didn't know whether he could deliver on. Not with the things he'd witnessed, growing up, not with the life they led now.

'I'll try questioning Hanely and Hallet, maybe that pastor, too, tomorrow. One of them might break.'

She nodded, disappointment in her eyes, but also resignation. 'I'll take the newspaper-man's wife, then some of the bargals at night.'

The jealous glint came back to his eyes, but with it concern for her safety. 'This town at night ain't the best place for a woman...'

She smiled a weak smile. 'That makes it all the better knowing you got my back, too.' When he turned away, staring back out through the window, she folded the note and set it on the nightstand. 'How do you know this man isn't really that girl's killer? I mean, the handwriting looks like a fella with something on his conscience. Maybe he did kill her out of some rage and worry that his daughter would find out what he was doing.'

Jim turned from the window. 'No, he was murdered. Reckon if I compared that handwriting to something he actually wrote there'd be a big difference, but doesn't matter even if it were the same. Just means someone forced him to write it.'

'Reckon you got a good reason for thinking that?'

Head turning, he gazed at her. 'He supposedly blew two holes through his mouth. Gun was still in his hand. Plenty of black powder around his lips but not a speck I could see on his gun hand. He never fired that gun. Someone else put it in his grip after killing him.'

She nodded. 'You think it was either of those men?'

He shrugged. 'Not sure at this point.

Hallet's a mousy guy, more a follower type, I suspect, not one to actually do the dirty work. Hanely, he's stronger, but I don't see him as a killer, either.'

'Pastor Bill?'

His brow arched. 'You wouldn't think a man of the cloth would be suspect, would you? But that fella ... something about him ... think I've seen his face somewhere before, too. Can't recollect where.' He turned back to the window.

Tootie came up behind him and slid her arms around his waist. As she pressed her cheek to his back shivers wandered over him. 'We'll find her killer, Jim.'

'Reckon.' His belly cinched and he wished – though not entirely – that she would go back to her room before he lost control of the man he fought to keep inside. Of all the dangers in his life, she was perhaps the most threatening, because she was the one danger he wanted desperately to surrender to. But Jim Hannigan just didn't do that. He never let down his guard, never let anyone too close.

He came from his thoughts with the soft click of the door closing. Turning, he found the room empty. Each time she left his presence, loneliness nearly crushed him, left a haunted feeling in his innards he couldn't figure. He wanted her distant, yet the moment she was it drove him crazy. He reckoned it wasn't a good sign.

Pastor Bill McKee gazed out through the church window, watching the revelers wreak havoc in the streets. With the dawn would come redemption, a never-ending cycle, and the thought brought a satisfied smile to his lips. The church was dark, the only light filtering through windows from hanging lanterns in the street. Shadows choked every corner and he felt at home within their embrace.

Lightning flashed and his eyes narrowed. For a moment he tensed, unmoving, as if in the grip of some dark spell. The lightning hadn't come from outside the church. It had sizzled from the turbulent depths of his mind.

Lightning. Long ago. Jagged claws of it. Scratching at a slate sky. And rain. Beating down. Soaking a boy of seven, a boy abandoned on a doorstep of a foundling home.

He was dark even then, though still throbbing with the wild exuberance of youth. But the last of that boyish innocence died that night, didn't it? *He* died that night, the

129

moment the sister opened the door and peered down with her stern eyes, then grabbed him with her beefy, spotted hands and dragged him into the home.

Abandoned.

A boy of seven with a whore for a mother who detested the very sight of the young son given to peculiar turns of cruelty with some of the street animals and kids his age or younger. If she had only known the true extent of his darkness, the beast waiting to awaken in the depths of his soul. But she hadn't known, because her nights were spent with nameless men and Doctor Laudanum. Why she kept him at all was a mystery to him still.

Just past his ninth birthday he snapped Jimmy Taylor's neck. For a spell he wondered whether one of the sisters would discover his deed, and it had filled him with a hot excitement that he could hardly contain.

The sisters had noticed his sullen turns, his sometimes vicious behavior when he thought they weren't looking. They fretted over it. They thought they could save his black soul and send him back out into the world a better and more godly human being. They thought they could do it by beating the devil out of him, showing him the Way, the Light, the difference between sin and salvation. It didn't take long before he no longer knew which part of him would be in control at any given moment.

He murdered his mother the moment he left the home. He murdered two of the nuns as well, the two who had beaten him the most, leaving their bodies hanging from rafters as beacons of God's righteous punishment. He thanked the others for the hatred and fury they'd burned into an already – what was the word they liked to use? Oh, yes: *Disturbed*. A disturbed child.

He formed his first gang not long after that. He was a natural leader, after all. Anyone who said different wound up lookin' at the inside of a coffin. Praise be.

Shots from outside pulled him from his dark thoughts. Ignoring them, he turned from the window. Such was life. And death. He had power over both in this town. He held sway over every man, woman and child and it swelled within him like an engorged black river.

Well, perhaps one man defied his rule, and that simply could not be allowed. He recognized the name of Jim Hannigan. What man on the owlhoot didn't? Hannigan was dangerous, perhaps the most dangerous of all his type. Would he believe Quimby to be guilty of murder and leave Revelation Pass? Slight chance, he figured, but worth trying. If Hannigan refused to leave, something more substantial would have to be done. Too much was at stake, too much money involved, to let one man ruin it all, no matter how much reputation he carried.

'Vengeance is mine sayeth the Lord...' he whispered. 'Not yours, Mr Hannigan.'

His mind faded for an instant, lost in some dark world of his past. Anger came at the challenge to his control in the form of a manhunter. When the shadowy outlines of pews came back into focus before him again he could barely contain the fury surging through his nerves. He forced a deep breath, suppressing the rage with the thought of a face. Another new soul in town, a woman. He'd seen her walking into the hotel when he was shadowing Hannigan. She was different. She intrigued him, reminded him of one of the nuns he had cornered one night in the dark of the foundling-home grounds. Perhaps another early lottery was in order. He knew full well those two fools often doctored the names they drew so that a traveler would be given over unto him, instead of one of their precious own. Perhaps this one he'd save for himself, instead of sending her on.

In the darkness he smiled. Then his mind again wandered through the dark corridors of the past.

CHAPTER SEVEN

With the sunrise the streets of Revelation Pass returned to their queer calmness. Jim Hannigan surveyed the street as he stepped from the hotel, eyes narrowing in befuddlement. He reckoned he'd never seen the likes and last night's revelry just made the situation all the more bizarre.

The sun blazed like a ball of brass, its light glinting from windows where workers industriously scoured away all traces of liquor splashed on the panes by drunkards. Women in high-collar day-dresses swept debris on the boardwalks into small piles, then scooped it into buckets, which men hauled away. Cowboys who had passed out on the streets were carried off. Shop owners swabbed walls and floors. Others replaced broken signs and rails at an efficient, furious pace that indicated they had done it countless times before. No sign remained of any of the bar-girls. All appeared serene, as if nothing had ever occurred on the previous night.

He stepped into the street. A man fixing a rail gave him one of the mechanically placid smiles and tipped a finger to his hat.

'You folks put on the elephant that way every night?' Jim asked and the man's expression didn't change. He simply ignored the question and went back to what he was doing.

Jim debated pushing the matter but reckoned he had more important things to do at this point than figure out why this town flipped-flopped from heaven to hell with the setting of the sun.

The heat was already strong enough to wither a fence post. A pencil-thin stream of sweat trickled down the side of his face as he walked across the street to the opposite boardwalk. His body ached from the fight and a night of fitful sleep. He'd replayed the events of the case in his mind a number of times, come no closer to answers. One dead woman who had met her doom for an unknown reason, by an unknown killer; a town that went to opposite ends of the spectrum in a heartbeat; a dead man, murdered, whom at least two others sought to brand as the young woman's killer. But did either Hallet or Hanely know that Quimby's death was not suicide? Or had they accepted the note at face value?

Hannigan wouldn't let either off the hook at this point. He pegged them as liars, possibly accomplices, but not the murdering type. That being the case, whom did that leave, pulling their strings?

A name came to mind, but a measure of doubt gripped him at linking a man of the cloth to murder. Still, Pastor Bill made every one of Hannigan's manhunter nerves stand on end. He wagered there was more to the man than met the eye. From seeing the men briefly interact, Hannigan judged Hallet and Hanely were intimated by the preacher. Quimby even more so.

Had the girl's murder remained solitary, Hannigan might have begun looking at the possibility that it was a random act in a rowdy cowtown, in light of last night's debauchery. But Quimby's death was too convenient; it pointed to one conclusion: someone didn't want him investigating any further, had decided to make things easy for him. Two murders, at least one calculated.

Why Quimby? Hannigan figured he knew.

Quimby looked ready to break down yesterday. The killer realized that, had seized on an opportunity to kill two birds with one stone.

Who?

Again Pastor Bill's name rose in his mind.

He sighed. What possible motive would a preacher have for killing a young woman and leaving her body hanging at the entrance to town? Then murdering Quimby to cover it up?

''Less he ain't a real preacher...' Hannigan mumbled. The flash of familiarity made him wonder if Bill's face had appeared on a dodger he'd seen somewhere and paid no attention to while searching posters for some outlaw. A longshot, but at some point soon, or if Tootie had no luck in questioning Hallet's wife or the bargals, he would break into the boarded-up marshal's office and see whether there weren't some old posters lying about. Maybe he would wire his Pinkerton contact about the man as well, but first he needed a last name on Pastor Bill.

On reaching the bank, he came from his thoughts and entered the building. The lobby was cooler, heavy with the odor of old bills and paper. A row of barred teller-cages stood to the left, employees working at their stations. Near the back squatted a huge desk fashioned of dark wood. Behind the desk sat Bertrim Hanely.

Hannigan's boots clacked on worn tiles as he crossed the lobby to Hanely's desk. A gold name-plate indicated the bank man's name and position as manager, and the blotter was stacked with papers. Hanely didn't appear to notice him for a moment, then looked up with a start.

'Mr Hannigan...' His voice came a notch too high. 'I was hoping you'd be on your way by now.'

Hannigan gave him a vague smile. 'Reckon you were.'

Hanely sighed. 'I don't understand. You have your killer and the suicide note gives you all the proof you need.'

Hannigan leaned over Hanely's desk, both hands gripping the edge. 'I got to thinkin', Mr Hanely. I got to thinkin' that if I were to compare that note with a sample of Quimby's handwriting there'd be a difference.'

Hanely blinked but Hannigan had to give him credit for keeping his composure, if indeed he were somehow involved in the shopkeep's death. 'That what you were getting at last night when you asked me if Quimby had a loan with the bank? You wanted to compare it?'

Hannigan nodded. 'Reckon I could go over to his store now and find some slip or memo he signed. What do you think I'd discover if I were to do that, Hanely?'

Hanely's tongue probed at the inside of his cheek and he remained silent for a moment. 'I think you would find Mr Quimby was a disturbed man carrying a bellyful of guilt. I think he had very little control over his senses and his handwriting at the point he shot himself, and that means any variance in his writing is perfectly understandable.'

Hannigan straightened. 'I think you're a damned poor liar, Mr Hanely.'

'Now see here!' The bank man's face went a shade of red that Hannigan found particularly satisfying. If he were going to force a slip, he needed to shake up the man.

'No, you see here, Mr Hanely. Quimby didn't kill himself. Someone did that for him, likely because whoever it was wanted to cover up that girl's murder and knew Quimby was a risk for telling something he knew. Only three other men besides myself saw how shaken up that man was yesterday when I brought the body in.'

'You have no call saying that. No evidence.' The confidence had trickled out of Hanely's tone.

'You ever fire an over-under .44, Mr Hanely? Especially a homemade version? Quite a backblow on them. Sometimes the damn thing will even misfire the second barrel once the first goes off.'

'I don't see how that has any bearing on Quimby's death.'

'Quimby's mouth showed some residue but his hand was clean, Mr Hanely. He didn't fire that gun. Someone else fired it, then placed it in his hand after he was dead. Would you like me retrieve the gun and prove it to you?'

Hanely peered at the manhunter, unsure whether a threat came with the question. 'I accept Mr Quimby's confession and suicide, Mr Hannigan. I know nothing of powders and what an insane man might be capable of when taking his own life.'

Hannigan held the banker's gaze. 'And again I'd call you a liar, Hanely. Who wanted Quimby dead before he slipped and told something?'

'No one. No one wanted him dead.'

'Who killed that girl and left her hanging, Mr Hanely?' Hannigan's tone raised a notch.

'I told you, Quimby—'

'Who is Pastor Bill, Mr Hanely?'

'P-pastor Bill? What—'

139

'Is he involved in this somehow? Does he pull your strings, Mr Hanely? Hallet's? Did he pull Quimby's?'

'Now see here, Hannigan!' Hanely came from his chair, but kept a respectable distance from Hannigan to prevent the manhunter from grabbing him. Tellers behind their cages looked over at the raised voices, their faces fraught with curiosity and concern. 'You cannot just go accusing a respectable citizen of some terrible deed, not in this town.'

'Can't I, Mr Hanely? You got no law here. Seems like I can do whatever I damn well please, 'less you got someone else who can stop me.'

Hannigan held Hanely's gaze and the man's eyes registered worry and confusion. He didn't know how to react to Hannigan's flurry of questions, but it wasn't going to break him. Hannigan could see that. Something else held the man in check, perhaps fear that the same thing that happened to Quimby would happen to him.

'Pastor Bill is a man of the cloth, sir.' Hanely lowered himself back into his chair, as if his willpower had deserted him, his rage a paper tiger. 'He has done nothing but good for this community.'

140

Hannigan folded his arms. 'Why do I get the notion you don't believe that yourself, Hanely?'

'You misread me, Hannigan.'

'Do I?' His eyebrow arched. 'I doubt it. What happened to your law here anyway, Mr Hanely?'

Hanely's eyes shifted and worry bled back into his expression. 'He ... left.'

'Just rode on out?'

'I reckon that's what it was.'

Hanely was lying. ''Bout the time Pastor Bill came to town by any chance?'

Hanely remained silent but a flinch of his facial muscles gave away the answer.

'Your lawman's dead, ain't he?'

Hanely's gaze dropped, then came back up. 'Was an accident. He fell off his horse and broke his neck.'

Hannigan let out a small sound of disgust. 'Dangerous business being in a saddle.'

Hanely's lips pinched into a pained frown. He made a motion with his hand at the tellers, who quickly returned to their business. Customers were filtering in, vacuous expressions riding their faces. Hannigan glanced at them, then back to the banker.

'What is it with this town, Mr Hanely? Why is it so damned tranquil during the day

141

and rowdy at night?'

Hanely cleared his throat. 'That's just the way it is, Mr Hannigan.'

Hannigan unfolded his arms, a frown turning his lips. He was getting damned tired of non-answers. 'Because Pastor Bill says so?'

He had hit the mark. Hanely almost nodded, but caught himself. 'If you have no further need to harass me, I have a bank to run.'

Hannigan leaned over the desk, face close to Hanely's. 'I aim to find that girl's killer. That means tearing this town apart piece by piece and finding out the truth 'bout whatever it is you folks got going on here, I'll do it. Be a lot easier on us all if you decide to come clean.'

Hanely let out a long breath, his demeanor softening a measure. 'Please, Mr Hannigan, we don't need more death here. That poor girl and Quimby were enough. Don't stir up trouble. Just leave us be and let us live the only way we can.'

Hannigan heard a plea in the man's voice that went beyond his words. It was the first measure of sincerity he'd seen from the man. Straightening, he tipped a finger to his hat and left the banker sitting at his desk, face in his hands.

Hannigan entered the newspaper office to the tang of ink and fresh paper. As his gaze scanned the room he spotted the mousy man arched over a table, arranging slips of paper. At a small desk sat Tootie, her Hannah Garret disguise a hell of a lot less revealing than the bargal get-up. He almost smiled at that thought. She glanced up at him, then lowered her eyes. At a back table a heavyset woman was piling a stack of papers into a wooden crate. She gazed at Hannigan with a look of curiosity, and nodded a greeting.

Hallet looked up at last as Hannigan came towards him. The expression on his face jumped from surprise to irritation mixed with trepidation in a blink. He wasn't made of the same stuff as Hanely, that was obvious. Hannigan hoped his tactics would prove more effective on a man of lesser character.

'Reckon your morning edition will carry the news of Mr Quimby's murder...' Hannigan put a slight emphasis on the word 'murder', watching closely for the newspaperman's reaction.

Hallet's brow cinched. 'Murder? I instructed Miss Garret to write the report of poor Quimby's ... demise, but it was no murder, Mr Hannigan. Quimby killed that

143

poor girl, then himself. Simple as that, sir, simple as that.'

Hallet's speech was a notch too fast, his tone a bit wobbly. 'Best check with Hanely on that, Mr Hallet. I just stopped by the bank, told him plain Quimby's death wasn't by his own hand.'

'That's simply ridiculous. Why concoct such a tale, Mr Hannigan?'

Hannigan smiled to himself at hearing a hitch in Hallet's voice. 'You're a newspaperman. I assume you check your facts before you print them? Ask the funeral-man about Quimby's clean hands and the mess a .44 over-under would make firing.'

Hallet started, confirming instantly that he knew exactly what the manhunter was talking about. He might have given Hanely the benefit of the doubt when it came to weapons, but Hallet damn well knew about guns, that was plain to see.

'It might have been a freak thing...' Hallet's voice carried little confidence. He was scrambling to think of something, but coming up empty.

'You're familiar with firearms, aren't you, Mr Hallet?'

'My cousin, Frisk, makes all–' Hallet stopped suddenly, as if afraid he had just implicated himself inadvertently. Hannigan saw panic jump about in his eyes.

'Reckon your cousin made that derringer, then. You might have told me that last night.'

Hallet looked back to his paper-clippings, hands fumbling with the slips. 'Didn't see no point in it. Don't matter who makes guns. Anybody could buy a gun from my cousin.'

'You saying anybody could have killed Quimby?'

Hallet's gaze returned to Hannigan with a glint of defiance. 'Hell, no! I just meant Quimby must have bought it from him.'

'Maybe I should ask your cousin if he sold Quimby a derringer or whether he sold one to someone else?'

Hallet's face shaded crimson. 'Just who the devil do you think you are, Hannigan? What right you got riding into our town and accusing folks of things?'

'Don't recollect accusing anyone of anything yet, Mr Hallet. You got a guilty conscience?' Hannigan noticed Tootie's gaze flick to them and the woman at the back stood staring, making no move to intervene, though he saw something close to panic on her features.

Hallet remained silent, but the crimson on

his face deepened nearly to purple.

'Maybe you went to your cousin and bought a derringer, Mr Hallet. Maybe you went to visit Quimby, shoved a gun in his mouth and pulled the trigger. How 'bout it, Mr Hallet? Your hands stained with powder and blood?'

Automatically, Hallet glanced down at his hands, which were stained with ink but nothing else. He caught himself, locked gazes with Hannigan. 'Get the hell out of here, Hannigan. You got no call coming in here and spewing such nonsense, no call.'

Hannigan stepped closer to the man, getting in his face. 'I got every call, Hallet. I think you got a hell of a lot more interest in this case than you want me to believe. I think Hanely does, too, and likely so did Quimby and that's why he's dead.'

Hallet tried to back away, but the table blocked him. Flecks of spittle gathered at the corner of his mouth and his bravado melted. 'Q-Quimby was my friend...'

'That so? You treat all your friends to lead, Hallet?'

'I didn't kill him. I didn't kill him!' Tears gathered in the newspaperman's eyes and his body shook.

Hannigan backed off a step, deciding not

to break Hallet at this point, maybe just frighten him enough to scurry for help from whoever pulled his strings. 'I find out you did, I'll be back for you, Hallet. That clear?'

Hallet stuttered a nod.

Hannigan backed to the door, keeping his sights on the newspaperman, who seemed to be using the table to keep himself from crumpling to the floor. He'd given Hallet some rope, now to see if he hanged himself with it. 'You have a change of heart, Hallet, you can find me around.'

Hallet stared, as if frozen.

Hannigan tipped a finger to his hat at Tootie and the heavyset woman, then left the newspaper office, a bit more satisfied than when he'd departed from the bank.

Tootie watched Hannigan leave, then shifted her gaze to John Hallet. She didn't like him, not one bit. Something about him made her think of a weasel. She had decided to leave him mostly to Hannigan, because his type would likely cave in fast to intimidation but the little *hombre* figured himself a ladies man, that was plain, so it left her an ace if Hannigan's method failed. The thought made her want to shiver.

Hallet stood immobile for long moments,

then without a word walked stiff-legged to the back room. She almost smiled.

Turning, she glanced at Bertha, who returned to piling newspapers in a crate. The older woman's features had pulled into stern lines, painted with worry. Despite a brusque demeanor, Tootie pegged Bertha as more compassionate than her husband. They seemed an odd match. The talk between the two was casual, more like what she would have expected from acquaintances instead of husband and wife. And the bruises on Bertha's face ... she wagered Hallet had put them there.

Tootie laid her quill pen on the desktop and stood, smoothing her dress-front, then casually made her way to the back to stand beside Bertha.

'I finished the write-up for tomorrow's edition,' she said.

Bertha nodded. 'Mrs Grumpet's fixin' to pass along her apple-pie recipe at the fair end of August. I'll have you stop by her place and interview her about it.'

How exciting, she thought, but kept the sarcasm off her face. 'That man who was just in here...'

Bertha's face tightened. 'What about him?'

'Who was he?'

'Hannigan, heard he was. Stranger.'

'I declare, he seemed such an awful man, the way he treated poor Mr Hallet.'

Something close to a smile flickered on Bertha Hallet's face. 'He'll live.'

Tootie studied the older woman, her impression that she and her husband weren't close strengthening. 'But he seemed frightened half to death. Perhaps I should go talk to him?'

A dark cloud swept across Bertha's expression. 'Stay away from John, deary. A good whupping might do him good.'

'I don't understand.'

'No, you don't, and you don't want to. Please, just take my advice and don't talk to him more than you have to. In fact, might be best if you consider finding yourself another town and moving on.'

'But I just arrived. You just hired me.' Tootie feigned concern over her job, but she saw no jealously or threat in the woman's manner, heard none in her voice. A different emotion came with her words: concern. She was directing Tootie away from this town in an attempt to keep her from some harm.

Bertha sighed. 'You're a pretty girl, smart, too. You can do better. Find yourself a young fella and settle down. This town ain't no place for a gal like you.'

Tootie touched her splayed fingers to her bosom and worked a look of surprise. 'My, is there something here that might bring me harm? I heard a considerable amount of noise outside the hotel last night. I declare, I was so frightened I pulled the covers right over my little old head.'

Bertha shrugged and stacked a few more papers into the crate. Tootie didn't think she was going to say anything further, but the woman peered at her, looking suddenly ten years older. 'Don't go out at night, deary. Lock your door and stay inside. Things go on at night in this town no decent girl like yourself wants any part of.'

'Why, Miss Bertha, you're frightening me so. What kind of things?'

Bertha shook her head. 'I've said too much already. Please, just do what I tell you and don't ask no more questions about it.'

Tootie nodded, backing away as Bertha went back to her duty.

Lowering herself into her seat, Tootie took her pen and doodled on a slip of paper, wondering just what the older woman was getting at. Did she know something more? Was she merely worried about a girl's welfare in a town where all hell broke lose at night? Or did her warning have a deeper meaning?

Tootie's head lifted slightly and she cleared her throat. Without turning, she asked: 'The girl who used to work here...'

Bertha looked up from her newspapers. 'Miss Quimby.'

The name startled Tootie but she didn't let it show. 'Was that Mr Quimby's wife?' She turned to look at Bertha.

The older woman shook her head. 'No, his daughter.'

'What happened to her? Why did she quit?'

This time sadness flooded the older woman's eyes. 'She ... she just left.'

'Left? Where did she go?'

'She moved on with some fella,' a voice said from the back, as Hallet returned from the back room, looking only a hair more composed. Sweat soaked his shirt and his face had drained of any color. His tone carried a clipped edge. He looked at Tootie, as if trying to fathom something behind her question. 'You best attend to your work and stop bothering with things that aren't your concern.'

Bertha averted her eyes and Tootie nodded, turning back to her desk.

Hallet moved towards the door.

'Where are you going?' asked Bertha, not bothering to look at him.

'None of your goddamn business, woman.' Hallet stepped outside, slamming the door behind him.

A small smile filtered onto Tootie's lips. She was willing to bet the fish was going for the worm.

Hannigan had waited just beyond the corner of an alley running beside the newspaper office for the past fifteen minutes. He'd begun to think Hallet hadn't swallowed the bait, or that perhaps he had overplayed his hand and frightened the man into staying put for the time being. He breathed a relieved sigh when the office door popped open and the mousy fellow stepped out onto the boardwalk, face an irritated mask. Hannigan moved back into the alley a bit as Hallet's gaze swept in all directions. Likely he never gave a thought to being followed, but was looking over his shoulder out of habit, which strengthened the manhunter's suspicions further.

The newspaperman scurried along the boardwalk, pausing only briefly when folks stopped to wish him good morning. He labored to paste one of the phony smiles onto his face, but appeared too agitated to pull it off.

Hallet practically skidded to a stop, then darted into a shop, which carried a hanging sign that read: Frisk, Gunsmith. The stop confirmed that Hallet either had purchased the derringer himself or knew who had, and had decided to warn his cousin not to disclose the information to anyone who asked. Hannigan decided not to confront the gunsmith immediately after Hallet's departure. He was more interested in where the newspaperman went next.

Twenty minutes later the mousy newspaperman stepped out into the sunlight, appearing a notch more relaxed. He sauntered along the boardwalk towards the town fork, looking for all the world like a man who'd just managed to button his britches before his tallywacker fell out.

Four blocks down, Hallet reached his destination and a grim smile forced itself onto Hannigan's lips. The church, a whitewashed building of wood and brick, had a sign before it painted with gold lettering in gothic type that read: Revelation Church.

Hallet glanced about, nodding to passersby, then climbed the steps and vanished into the church. Hannigan didn't need to be a fortune-teller to guess whom the newspaperman intended to meet. It made him all the more certain Pastor Bill was up to his collar in something irreverent. He debated getting close enough to overhear their conversation, but too many people wandered about and he saw no place in which to conceal himself.

With a prickle of frustration, he decided to wait until Hallet finished, then figure out the next course of action. He backed to the corner of a building and folded his arms, jamming a shoulder to the wall. An antsy feeling skittered through his nerves. He'd never been good at sitting still, but for the moment he saw little choice.

Pastor Bill knelt at the altar, gazing ahead as if in a trance. His thoughts wandered along the dark passages of his mind, reveling in the gratification he felt from his power over this town and the lucrative operation he'd built here. The Almighty had truly blessed him, yes, indeed, yet something was missing, something that would complete his reign. A woman, perhaps...

The door jerking open behind him pulled him from his thoughts. With a prickle of annoyance he rose, turned to see Hallet bounding down the aisle. Hallet. Such an pathetic little toad. Eager – too eager – to please. Hallet fancied he would earn himself favors from them for his part in the scheme, but the newspaperman was sadly mistaken. As a lackey, he had his uses, but eventually the time would come to leave him bleeding in the dust. Bill would enjoy that. He detested the sniveling coward. In fact, it would have been so much more satisfying had Hallet been the one on the verge of breaking instead of Quimby. Quimby was spineless in his way, but less like the groveling little puppy begging to be kicked.

'Brother Hallet, what brings you to the House of the Lord on this fine morning?' Bill's face composed itself into the beatific expression he'd worked so long to perfect.

'Hannigan came to see me. He knows Quimby didn't kill himself.' The words tumbled out in a connected stutter.

Pastor Bill nodded, a small frown spoiling the angelic mask. He couldn't say it was unexpected. Hannigan wasn't stupid. He hadn't forged his reputation by following false trails, but Bill had hoped for the slim chance that the manhunter would accept the easy solution. That was the trouble with men of character; they seldom took the cleared trail. 'Why, Brother Hallet, that is indeed distressing news. Are you certain?'

Hallet nodded a rabbit nod. 'He noticed

Quimby's hands were clean of powder, figured out he didn't pull the trigger himself. He accused me of buying the derringer from Frisk.'

Bill's gaze lifted, looking past Hallet at the way the sunlight streamed through the windows in dusty rays, fell in peculiar patterns along the worn floor. For an instant dark things dwelled within those patterns, reaching out for him. He sighed. 'Then we must speak to Mr Frisk and make certain he doesn't provide Mr Hannigan with any information.'

'Already did. I told him Hannigan might drop by askin' questions, told him to make up some sort of story about Quimby buying the gun himself.'

'You've done well, Brother Hallet. Our Mr Hannigan is certainly a problem. I will take it into consideration.'

Hallet's face beamed with the praise. 'There's one more thing...'

Bill forced the angelic expression back onto his features. 'Mr Hallet, you certainly are God's messenger today.'

'I heard the new gal we hired askin' on Quimby's daughter.'

Bill's eyebrow arched. 'Perhaps she was merely curious about the woman who formerly held her job.'

Hallet nodded. 'Reckon that was it. But I thought it best you knew. She wanted to know where Miss Quimby got off to. I told her she ran off with some fella.'

It was closer to the truth than Hallet likely thought. 'Very well, Brother Hallet. If you should learn anything further…'

'Sure thing, Pastor. You can count on me.'

'I expect you'll be attending Sunday service as usual?'

'I'll be there. I'll be there. Hanely, too. We never miss it.'

'Only sinners do, Mr Hallet. You are not a sinner, are you?'

'No, no sir. Reckon I'm not.' Hallet backed away, looking suddenly uncomfortable and likely figuring that remaining any longer would overstretch his welcome. Bill watched the man scurry from the church, considering the information the newspaperman had brought. Hannigan was definitely a danger; something would have to be done.

And the new girl. That was likely nothing. Still, perhaps a visit was in order.

'You give me the willies when you talk all that God-fearing stuff, McKee.'

Pastor Bill turned to see the hardcase with the scar coming from the back room.

'The spirit was with me.' A memory careened through his mind and he felt the nun striking him across the face with the switch. He flinched, a small sound escaping his lips. The switch came down again and again, until his cheeks bled and whatever mistake he'd made – he couldn't even recollect anymore – was beaten out of him.

'McKee?'

Bill's gaze focused on Bartlett, who peered at him with a peculiar, wondering expression. 'You heard?'

Bartlett nodded. 'I heard. We're gonna have to take care of Hannigan if this keeps up. He ain't like to drop it.'

'No, I don't believe he is. Best move on him. Likely Hannigan set up that idiot Hallet and was led straight here.'

Bartlett folded his arms. 'When?'

'I'll be giving a sermon in the street tomorrow. Arrange something for then. He's like to want to be there. I got a notion he'll be lookin' to put a noose around my neck. He doesn't know who I am yet, but he'll figure it out. Meantime, go over to the gunsmith and cancel our account. Don't need that idiot spilling to Hannigan I bought that derringer.'

Bartlett nodded. 'Heard from Willis. Riders will be here in two days for the shipment. Got a rich chilli-eater lookin' for some white meat.'

The smile came back to Bill's lips. 'He's paying exorbitantly, of course?'

'Near enough to end this operation and move on.'

'Why would we do that, Bartlett? I quite like it here. My flock is here.'

Bartlett stared at Bill as if wondering something, and the preacher didn't care for it. It was the same look the hardcase had given him when he was instructed to hang that girl at the edge of town, one that asked if Bill had come out of his saddle.

'Things have died down. No one's looking for us anymore–'

'Someone will always be looking for us, Bartlett, even if it's a fella like Hannigan who don't realize it yet. Do what you're told. You question my orders again and there'll be another body hanging from that tree.'

The hardcase's mouth pinched, but he remained silent, then returned to the back. Bill stood still a moment, again watching the sunlight and shadows interact, then strolled toward the front doors. In some secret part of his mind he fought the gnawing suspicion that Bartlett's questioning looks might be justified, that some of his control over the fury within himself had slipped and would continue to do so. Hanging that girl was a stupid move, but he hadn't been able to stop himself. He couldn't even tell why he'd ordered it done. It just pleased him, frightening his flock into compliance. Bill McKee was a man who did whatever pleased him. And would again.

Tootie gathered up her pad, quill-pen and bottle of ink, then headed for the door. Bertha had assigned her an interview with Mrs Grumpet but discovering the minutiae of apple-pie baking excited her about as much as had sitting behind the desk for the past few hours. If she had learned one thing it was that Tootie del Pelado was a gal of action.

Unfortunately the assignment also prevented her from being much help to Hannigan, though she wagered he'd be grinning that smug look of his if he had known she was stuck writing about pies. He worried about her, she knew that. Inordinately, as of late, but in a way she liked it. A lot. It expressed more about his feelings than he cared to put into words. She'd never had anyone to worry over her and the notion made her innards warm. If only he'd come right out and say it.

Sighing, she opened the door and stepped into the late morning sunlight, knowing there was no use in going over it again. She couldn't force him; he'd just retract further.

Jerked from her thoughts suddenly, a startled gasp escaped her lips. She stopped just short of running into a man standing outside the newspaper office. Backing off a step, her eyes narrowed and she forced the fluster from her features.

'My dear young lady, I find I must apologize for frightening you so.' Pastor Bill's features oiled with a beatific expression that she reckoned could only come to a man hiding something. She'd seen the look before; it always meant a concealed agenda.

She cast him a glare that said he had no call frightening a poor Southern belle half to death and silently called him a name Hannigan would have been shocked to discover she knew.

She batted her eyes and fanned her face with her pad. 'My good man, I do declare, you frightened me half out of my wits!'

He bowed curtly. 'Again, my apologies. I heard we had a lovely young woman in town and simply wanted to stop by and extend my warmest welcome.'

She tried to blush, wasn't sure if she

pulled it off, then curtsied. 'Why, suh, I do believe you flatter me.' Behind her ruse, she sized him up, studying the nuances of his manner, the way his affected demeanor covered a peculiar – what? She couldn't be certain. Maybe it was the blankness in his eyes, the one thing he couldn't disguise, like a spider's eyes peering out from a kitten, but he made her want to recoil.

'I meant no offense, my dear woman.' Slithery tone with a hint of unevenness; it reminded her a loco killer she'd encountered once on a case, but it clashed with the collar at his neck. Stepping closer, his hand drifted to her cheek and she fought the urge to jump back. 'Such a pretty young thing. I do hope you'll visit the church for Sunday service.'

His touch sent chills cascading through her innards and unearthed a dark memory. A time long ago, a man who'd visited the foundling home, a fellow who seemed so outwardly harmless, who brought baked goods from his local shop for all the girls. Girls he spent time with alone, substituting for fathers they no longer had. Or so she thought until the day he came to her room and caught her by herself. With a welling of nausea she recollected the yeasty odor and taste to his palm as he jammed a hand over her mouth while his other hand wandered over her dress front. She couldn't scream, couldn't move.

Only the approaching footsteps of some of the other girls had saved her from whatever fate he'd intended, but he'd threatened to kill her if she ever said anything. At fourteen, she'd been too scared to open her mouth. Over the next year, she'd avoided being anywhere near whenever he came by. Not long after that year passed, he was said to have left town, just ahead of a lynch-mob headed by a father whose fifteen-year-old daughter had screamed bloody hell in his shop when an errand to pick up fresh bread had turned into a ripped dress and unwanted advances. After Tootie joined the agency in New Mexico her first case involved tracking a man who'd raped a young woman. That fella had turned out to be the same man from the bakery. Last she heard a judge ordered him hanged.

This man reminded her of that fella. The thought made her shudder. He gazed at her, perplexed by her reaction, possibly angered.

She barely recovered her voice. 'My, my, I seem to have experienced a sudden chill, suh. I may just be coming down with the grippe.'

His expression relaxed. 'I'm sure you are

163

merely still exhausted from your journey. I expect we will see each other again?'

She wanted to say she hoped he got stomped on by a horse before that happened, but had the gnawing suspicion they would meet again and it wouldn't be on friendly terms. She curtsied and strolled away, feeling his eyes burn into her back. A block down, she noted Hannigan standing just inside an alley, leaning against the wall. He'd been watching. This time he had her back and the knowledge brought a measure of comfort, though the bad memory combined with the pastor's touch had shaken her more than she would have thought possible. Maybe she had a few things to learn about herself after all.

CHAPTER EIGHT

By the time Tootie took her place on the floor, rowdy cowhands and scattered hard-cases jammed the saloon. Her earlier encounter with Pastor Bill had percolated from disgust to anger. Like Hannigan, she tagged him as a major player in the strange events unfolding in Revelation Pass. Hannigan had given her his report on following John Hallet to the gunsmith's, then to the church. After leaving the reverend, the newspaperman had settled in a café a block down, so the man-hunter had waited, this time turning the tables on the preacher and trailing him to the newspaper office. The reverend's encounter with Tootie proved to be no chance meeting; he'd lingered outside the office until she came out.

Did he suspect her of working with Hannigan? Had Hallet overheard enough of her conversation with Bertha to raise his suspicions and send him running straight to the pastor with the news? If that were the case, she'd have to be extra careful that no one saw Hannah Garret go into the hotel and Tootie del Pelado come out.

She scanned the room, spotting no sign of Jenkins or Jasper among the crowd, all of whom appeared intent on mauling doves, gulping whiskey, or playing cards. She'd likely have to fend off her share of cowboys before the night was through. The absence of the two hardcases put a hold on the plan she'd been mulling to get one of them liquored up and talking, so she decided to modify her strategy and go with Plan B.

Her gaze skipped over the doves working

165

the room. After weighing personalities of the gals she'd scrutinized last night, she settled on one named Bayna as the talker of the bunch. Bayna hit a whiskey-bottle like a newborn calf gulping at a teat. The more she drank, the chattier she became.

Tootie spotted the young woman leaning against the end of the bar, a bottle in hand she'd pried from a cowboy just before he passed out and tumbled off his chair. He still lay on the floor, garnering the occasional kick from one of the patrons. Bayna brayed a laugh at each kick and chased it with another swig of redeye.

Arrowing towards the woman, Tootie threaded her way through tables and groping cowhands, swatting anyone who laid a hand on her person. Bayna appeared years older than she likely was, crevices around her mouth and eyes barely concealed under a heavy pancake of coral, kohl and powder. Tight ringlets of auburn hair spilled about her face, poodle-like. Her nose, large and fleshy, had obviously been broken at some point in the past, mending with a harsh crook to the left. With thin lips and brows that nearly touched in the center, she wasn't a looker, which was probably why she spent more time with bottles than marks.

Reaching the bar, Tootie leaned her back against its edge, glancing out at the barroom, then casting a casual look at Bayna. 'Tough night, uh?'

'Honeybun, they's all tough nights in this town.' Bayna surveyed her with a look of disapproval. 'You're the new one, ain't ya?'

'Second night, sweetie.' Tootie sprinkled sugar on her tone. 'Damn near didn't come in, though.'

Bayna cocked an eyebrow, giving the impression that that would have played just fine by her. 'Yeah? Why's that?'

'Well, heard about that gal that fella found hangin' outside of town. Figured maybe it wasn't safe bein' out at night.' It wasn't the smoothest lead-in she'd come up with, but she reckoned Bayna was too plied to notice.

Bayna brayed a laugh. 'You're joshin' me, right?'

'You ain't worried about someone killin' gals?'

'Hell, I ain't afeared of nothin', honeybun, but that ain't the point. You got nothing to worry about, either, 'less it's from some gal, if you try honin' in on her marks, you got my meanin'...?'

'I got it. You don't have to worry about me, sweetie. I'm just passin' through. Just need me enough money to get to the next town.' Tootie looked back to the barroom, giving the other woman a moment to finish pissin' on her territory. 'What did you mean, I got nothin' to worry about? Ain't all women gotta worry with some killer runnin' 'round these parts?'

Bayna peered at her, eyes glazed. 'Only those pretty young things gotta worry in this town, sugar. Not whores. They don't want whores.'

Tootie forced her voice to remain causal, though excitement surged through her veins. 'Who don't want whores?'

'Them that's takin' gals in Revelation Pass. They want young gals, pretty ones who ain't been deflowered yet.'

'Who's they exactly?'

The lines in Bayna's brow deepened. 'Don't know that.'

'How many gals been taken and killed?' Tootie angled towards Bayna, leaning a forearm on the bartop. Her gaze held the other dove's.

'Don't know if they been killed. Near a score, I'd reckon. Maybe more. Mostly gals stopping over for a spell.'

'How long's this been goin' on?'

Bayna shrugged, let out a belch. 'A spell,

maybe over a year, maybe two. Somethin' like that. Don't make me no nevermind. Whores are safe, that's all I care about. Fewer pretty gals in Revelation Pass the better, you ask me. Means more business.'

'Why'd that gal hang, then?'

'Don't know. Maybe she wasn't so pure and they didn't want her no more. Serves her right. She was too pretty. Pretty girls deserve whatever they get.' She gave Tootie a corrosive look of condemnation. Tootie ignored it.

'How'd you find this out, anyway? Maybe it's a tall tale.' Tootie put a measure of doubt into her voice, but not enough to brand the dove a liar and cap the well.

Bayna laughed again; it was as close to anything that came out of a donkey as Tootie had ever heard. 'We got a newspaperman in town who can't keep his tallywacker where it belongs. Damn fool spends money like redeye, though, and I give him a turn. He likes to talk.'

Tootie nodded, knowing exactly who the bargirl meant. 'Reckon he should know, being a newspaperman an' all.'

'What the hell's your name, anyway?' Bayna cocked an eyebrow and some of the glaze cleared from her eyes.

'Tootie.'

'Guess it ain't no mystery how you got that name. Well, Tootie, you listen to me. I'll put it to you straight – you stay away from my man and we'll get along just fine. I don't like pretty gals, sugar, but you keep that fancy little ass of yours outa my way and we'll get on just fine. You don't, you might find yourself hangin' longside that other gal.'

Tootie nodded, feigning a concerned expression. 'Like I said, I won't be here long. Just passin' through. I figure maybe somethin's wrong with this town.'

'Hell, this town's poison and virtuous gals pay the piper so's the rest of us can live peaceable.'

Tootie's brow cinched. 'What do you mean by that?'

Bayna's expression flashed to panic and Tootie felt certain the girl knew more about the disappearances than she was telling. Which meant Hallet knew more.

'Look, I ain't s'posed to be–' The panic turned to a look of sheer terror, but the dove tried to hide it. A shiver trickled down Tootie's spine as a hand touched her bare shoulder. She turned her head to look into the face of a man with a scar running from the tip of his nose to the lobe of his ear. Bayna's gaze riveted on him.

'Hope you ain't talkin' out of turn again, Bayna,' the man said, voice low and coarse. He rubbed Tootie's shoulder and she suppressed the urge to cringe.

'Hell, no, I ain't said nothin', Bartlett. Just makin' sure the new gal knows the ropes.' Her eyes averted from the hardcase's and she slipped away from the counter, taking her whiskey-bottle with her. Bartlett watched her go, hard eyes narrowed, suspicious. His gaze shifted to Tootie and she offered a coy smile.

'Let's you and me talk about spendin' some time together. I like to break in all the new gals...'

It occurred to her she was damn glad she had the derringer tucked into her bodice, because if he tried to take her upstairs she was going to blow off his pecans one at a time.

Dusk had swept across the town and already activity on the streets geared into full swing. Cowboys seemed to appear out of every nook and cranny, paying Jim Hannigan no attention as he headed for the gunshop.

He sauntered up to the shop door and leaned against the wall a few feet in front of it, intending to catch the owner, Hallet's cousin, as the man closed for the day and question him about the sale of the derringer. Twenty minutes passed. The shadows in the street darkened. Hanging lanterns came on. But no one came out of the shop.

Hannigan edged closer to the door, tried the handle. It turned in his grip and a quiver of alarm went through his belly. Pausing in the doorway, he found the interior dark, silent. Where was the owner? Why had he left the place open?

Glancing first into the darkened street to make sure no one had noticed or followed, he entered the shop and closed the door. Again he paused, listening. Nothing. A prickle of premonition raised gooseflesh on his arms. He moved deeper into the shop, alert, heart stepping up a beat. The smell of gunpowder and oil assailed his nostrils, along with it an odor like sour gunmetal.

Something in his belly twisted. Blood. The scent of blood.

As if in confirmation, his boot toe prodded something on the floor. Something soft, giving, yet heavy. Tensing, he fished in his pocket for a lucifer. The match flared and his gaze swept downward.

The body, a man's, lay in a pool of blood

that had half-soaked into the floorboards. The left side of the man's face was missing.

Hannigan dropped the match as it burned down. He lit another and squatted, studying the corpse. He reckoned Hallet's cousin wouldn't be making derringers for anyone ever again.

Straightening, he shook out the match and dropped it to the floor. No sense searching the place. He figured it right, whoever killed the gunsmith would have likely removed any record of sale.

Hallet? The newspaperman had come straight here earlier. But the manhunter doubted he had the balls to murder his own cousin.

That left another option: Hallet had told Pastor Bill about the derringer. Although Bill had gone to the paper to corner Tootie, he might have visited the shop later.

Or sent someone else to do the job.

Hannigan had no real proof, only suspicions, and pinning crimes on a man of the cloth was a dicey proposition. The uniform elicited a certain measure of respect and trust from most folks. In this case, he reckoned it provided camouflage, but he needed some sort of evidence if he were going to take the man in for murder.

Deciding he could do nothing further, he left the shop and headed for the saloon. Tootie would be in place by now. He worried that she might be in more danger after last night's fight. What if some hardcase had noticed her trying to help him and decided to keep an eye on her? The thought made his nerves tighten, but he tried to tell himself it was likely just his paranoia nettling him again. He couldn't help it and it just got worse as the weeks went on. He'd tried talkin' her out of going tonight but she had refused to listen.

You can't corral her, Hannigan. Not unless you're ready to give her what she wants and you're too damn mule-headed to do that. Even then, she ain't the type to be hogtied. She's your equal and you won't get away with treating her as anything less.

He pushed the thoughts from his mind as he reached the saloon. With a sigh, he stepped through the batwings and crossed the landing to the three steps leading to the saloon proper. Place was packed but he saw Tootie standing against the bar towards the back. A man stood next to her, a man whose hand suddenly clamped about her wrist. She struggled to pull free but he began dragging her towards a stairway that led to rooms above.

Hannigan's blood boiled and he took the steps in a single bound, then shoved through the sea of tables and people, cutting the two off before they reached the stairs.

'Let go of me, you sonofabitch!' Tootie's voice snapped out, almost a shout.

The man laughed, 'C'mon now, honey, I try out all the gals. You just gotta lay there and old Bart will do all the work.' He whirled her around into his arms and tried to kiss her. With a sudden yelp, he drew back, his lip gushing where she'd bitten a chunk out of it. She spat, fury widening her eyes, the muscles across her shoulders tensing for action. The hardcase let out a roar.

'You stupid little mattress-warmer–' He raised a hand to clout her. Tootie's hand whipped towards her bosom.

Hannigan moved forward a step, pivoted and got his arm up just as the hardcase's fist came down. The manhunter locked the 'case's forearm in the crook of his elbow and held it fast, pressing his face close to Bartlett's.

'That there's my gal for the night. I paid in advance, fella. You got a notion to get in the way?'

The scarred hardcase's eyes glittered with

175

fury and Hannigan readied for a fight. Seconds later the man's face eased a notch, fury boiling still, but a measure of rationality reining it in. He pulled his arm free of Hannigan's lock and backed away a step. Tootie glared, but her hand had come down to her waist.

'She's all yours, fella. Tomorrow's another day, though.' Bartlett flashed her a look, then swaggered off into the sea of tables, glancing back occasionally with spite.

Hannigan took Tootie by the wrist and led her towards the door. 'C'mon, wench, we got business.'

She let out a *pfft*. 'Wench? That'll cost you extra, mister. A *lot* extra...' She gave him a look that told him she'd let him have it for the remark later.

On reaching the boardwalk they headed towards the hotel. He released her wrist and she slipped an arm about his waist.

'Wench, eh?' A smirk pulled at her lips. 'Where'd you get that word, anyway?'

He suppressed a grin. 'Read it in a dime novel. Seemed like a good word.'

'Maybe we'll find out.' She giggled.

'Hallet's cousin's dead.'

Her face sobered. 'What happened?'

Hannigan explained what he'd discovered

when he entered the shop. 'Damned un-likely Hallet killed him.'

'Hallet's been busy with one of the whores in the saloon.' The young woman filled him in on what she'd learned from Bayna.

After she'd finished, Hannigan remained silent, trying to put the pieces of the mystery together in his mind. He didn't have enough yet, but he was more convinced than ever on one thing: 'Everything leads back to Pastor Bill somehow. I got a notion Hallet and Hanely work for him, or maybe do his bid-ding out of fear. Ties in with what your dove alluded to 'bout this town.'

'He's givin' a sermon in the street to-morrow,' Tootie said. 'When I got back from my interview, Bertha casually mentioned everyone in town was required to be there. He does it often. Preaches fire and brimstone during the day and lets sin run wild at night.'

Hannigan nodded. 'Maybe I best be there.'

She looked up at him. 'Maybe we best be there.'

'Thought you'd be trying out apple pie recipes.'

'That s'posed to be funny?'

'Reckon.'

'You reckon wrong.'

They walked in silence the rest of the way to the hotel. Most of the revelers ignored them, though a number of whores cast Tootie acidic glares. Hannigan had to admit that, though they were putting on an act to give him an excuse to bring Tootie into the hotel, he liked the feeling of her arm about him, her body next to his. He just wished it didn't scare the hell out of him at the same time.

They reached the hotel and entered the lobby. The counter was deserted, the clerk likely out with the revelers.

They made it to his room without encountering anyone.

Once inside, Hannigan lit the lanterns, then tossed his hat on a bedpost. 'Tomorrow, while the pastor gives his little speech, I'll get into the marshal's office and see what I can find for dodgers. I've seen that preacher's face somewhere before and I got a notion it wasn't on a church bulletin.'

Tootie nodded, going to the window and gazing out into the night. 'I thought I might try getting closer to Hallet, since he's got an eye for the ladies, but I ain't so sure after today. Lay a bet that pastor showed up 'cause the little sonofabitch overheard me askin' his wife about Quimby's daughter.

I'm sure he came to see if I presented any threat. Don't know what impression he came away with.' She paused. 'I got sloppy. I thought Hallet was too distracted after you came down on him. Should have waited till he left.'

'We've both made slips on this case, I reckon. Don't fret over it.' He wished he could convince himself of the same. It was one thing to risk his own life but another to place her in danger.

She turned to look at him, face a somber mask. 'We don't belong in this business if we're gonna start slippin' up. I ain't used to it. I've done this long enough to be damn good at it. I don't make mistakes.'

He shook his head. 'You're being too hard on yourself. I let men come up on me twice. Either time could have got me killed.'

'Why is that, Jim? You ever done that before Castigo Pass, before two months ago?'

He bowed his head, gaze searching the floor for nothing in particular. Christ, he hated it when she read him that way. She knew why he was distracted and had picked a hell of a time to press him on it.

'Tootie, we're just human. We make mistakes. Let it go at that.' His head lifted, but he avoided looking directly at her, knowing

179

she would force the truth out of him if he did.

A frown pulled at her lips. 'How long you figure on side-steppin' it? How long you think you got till it causes you to make some mistake that takes away the chance of ever having said the things you got to say to me? How long before you trust me?'

'I do trust you.'

'Not entirely.'

'That ain't true.' The words came out far weaker than he wanted them to.

Her lower lip began to tremble. 'You trust me with your life but you don't trust me with who you are. You think that if we keep going on cases you'll be able to avoid maybe the one thing in this world that scares you silly. But it's coming to an end, one way or the other, and you know it.'

He turned away, leaning a forearm against the bureau edge. Dammit, he didn't want to have this conversation now. He hadn't for two months, had become adept at avoiding it. She was right. If it got any worse, something would put an end to it, either a bullet or the cowardly move on his part he'd kept at the back of his mind over the past few weeks.

'I don't know if I can give you what you're

lookin' for, Tootie. I can't make you pro-
mises. I've seen what happens...'

For an instant he cringed with a memory
from long ago. A child, watching as a father's
fist came crashing down into a mother's
face. The shattered fragile features, drenched
in blood and–

Christ, *no*, he wouldn't let that memory
back in. Too many years he'd kept it down,
buried in the black depths of a ten-year-
old's nightmares.

'Tell me what happened, Jim.' Her voice
came soft, almost lulling, sapping some of
the pain from the memory. He wanted to
tell her, desperately wanted to. But could
not. He was a goddamned manhunter, an
instrument of vengeance, and they had a
girl's murderer to bring to justice. A girl
who might well have been the one in this
room under different circumstances. He
couldn't risk losing her that way.

*You'll lose her anyway, you damn fool, if you
don't say what you damn well know you need to
– what you want to.*

Mule-headed. That's what he was. No
question about it, but before he could stop
himself he had his mouth open and words
tumbled out. The wrong ones.

'I'll either find a warrant on Bill tomorrow

so I have something to base an arrest on, or I'll force something out of Hallet. You best stay away from the newspaper office tomorrow.' He couldn't look at her, couldn't face the hurt he knew was in her eyes.

She went to the door, pulled it open. 'Last time I checked we were partners. I don't take orders from you.' With a glance, he saw tears shimmering in her mahogany eyes, but she was too strong, too proud, to let him see her cry. She stepped out into the hall, softly shutting the door behind her and leaving him feeling suddenly more alone than he had ever felt in his life.

CHAPTER NINE

'It's not safe to meet here, especially in broad daylight.' Bertrim Hanely twisted at the watch chain dangling from his vest. He, John Hallet and Pastor Bill stood in the upstairs room of the general store. Sunlight streamed in a dusty shaft through the window, falling in amber ripples over the dried bloodstains on the table. Hanely fought to keep his focus off the stains, but the image of Quimby's gruesome corpse kept prying at his memory. 'Someone might see us.'

'Someone like Jim Hannigan perhaps, Brother Hanely?' Pastor Bill dragged his fingertips along the edge of the table. At the opposite side John Hallet shifted on his feet and bit at his lip.

'That's exactly who I mean.' Hanely's voice climbed in pitch. He saw everything coming to an end in a cascade of violence and stupidity. The preacher had clearly deteriorated mentally and couldn't distinguish idiocy from prudence.

'No one saw me come here, Brother Hanely. Please...' Bill's eyes narrowed, his face looking like an angelic skull. 'Refrain from taking that tone with me again. I would hate for God's wrath to fall upon you.'

A shiver threatened Hanely but he steeled himself and stiffened his carriage. 'There'll come a time when I'm not afraid to say my piece.'

A spark of rage flared behind the pastor's eyes. 'No, that time will never come, Brother Hanely. You know it and I know it. Because if that were to happen ... well, for the moment let's concentrate on more important matters.'

'What matters?' Hallet's gaze darted

between the men, the newspaperman obviously jittery as to how far Hanely was
willing to push Bill.

'Why, Brother Hallet, I have decided on
another lottery.'

'Another one?' Hanely's voice was laced
with incredulity. 'We've already had two this
week. You promised it would be monthly.
Just what the devil are you doing with all
these women, anyway? It isn't right.'

Bill's eyes narrowed a fraction. 'What I do
with them is of no concern to you, Brother
Hanely.'

Hanely noticed something as his gaze
flicked to Hallet, something he hadn't realized before. Hallet knew or strongly suspected what Bill was up to with those girls
and was keeping it to himself. Somehow he
had discovered something and never shared
it. Even now the glint of knowledge vanished
the moment Hanely's gaze fell upon him.
Hanely reckoned Hallet's impropriety with
bargirls had provided the little bastard with
insight into Bill's motives. Whores spilled
secrets, and Bill's hardcases were known to
frequent them.

Hanely's gaze shifted back to Bill, anger
simmering in his belly for Hallet, whom
he'd deal with when they were alone. 'You

can't ask us to give up another of our own. There won't be anything but whores left soon.'

Bill smiled the spider smile. 'Brother Hanely, I am not asking you to give up one of your own, not when you have a stranger in town, a Miss Hannah Garret. Brother Hallet was kind enough to inform me of her curiosity involving Miss Quimby, so I see no reason why she would not be a viable candidate for the lottery.'

'She works for the newspaper, for chrissakes. Only natural she'd ask questions. Doesn't mean she'll take it any further.'

Bill's voice evened, a note of exasperation creeping into it. 'No, I suppose she might not. But why take the risk?'

Hanely contemplated asking the bastard why he'd risked hanging a girl at the edge of town if he wasn't willing to let some innocent girl off the hook for innocuous questions. If the idiot hadn't lost his mind and hanged the Breck girl they might not be in this mess. They could have sent Hannigan on his way with nary a suspicion.

'It's broad daylight, for God's sake.' Hanely shook his head. 'I won't do it.' But he felt his strength wavering under the man's colorless glare.

'Certainly you will, Brother Hanely. It would be most inadvisable not to. In a few hours, I will be giving my sermon. You will wait until after I finish speaking. When the townspeople disperse, you and Brother Hallet will escort Miss Hannah Garret to the church. Inform her I wish to speak to her regarding Miss Quimby's *departure*.'

Hanely's belly plunged. 'What if she don't buy that? She could raise a ruckus and everyone would still be about.'

'The good folk of Revelation Pass will not bother you. You know that as well as anyone. And my men will be close by.'

Hanely sighed, defeat washing through him. 'What about Hannigan?'

'Mister Hannigan will meet with an unfortunate accident during the sermon.'

Nausea roiled in Hanely's gut. He doubted the manhunter would be that easy to kill. He wasn't like the lamebrained lawdog they'd had when this town was still known as Centerville. He peered at Bill with a notion to tell him he was plumb out of his saddle.

'You have something further to discuss, Brother Hanely?' The preacher's voice issued a challenge, one Hanely couldn't say he was up to. He cursed himself for being a coward.

'We'll get her to you, Pastor,' Hallet said, looking as eager as a puppy.

'I am most pleased to hear that, Brother Hallet. See that nothing goes wrong.' Pastor Bill smiled and left the room, the two men avoiding looking at each other after he departed. Then Hanely doubled over and vomited.

Jim Hannigan walked out of the hotel just as a crowd gathered to watch Pastor Bill mount an overturned crate and stretch his arms skyward in a melodramatic gesture of welcoming. A sea of blank expressions focused on the gaunt preacher, who pasted on his saintly mask and lowered his arms.

'My devoted brethren...' His voice came out as a soothing monotone, strangely hypnotic. Hannigan was forced to grant the man carried a certain power that was hard to resist, much like the spell of a snake about to devour a mouse.

'I welcome you, as followers in the Word, as sheep protected by the bonds of congreation and eternal reward. We are one body, united for the good of all. Our sins are forgiven through sacrifice, gladly given for the betterment of the whole.'

Hannigan suppressed the urge to scoff.

Was there a double meaning to the man's words? Did they link to missing girls, one confirmed dead, and two other murders? Hannigan's gaze roved over the sea of enraptured faces, spotting a number of hardcases embedded in the crowd. A tingle of alarm buzzed in his nerves, though none of the men appeared interested in him. All eyed the preacher. Yet he couldn't deny his manhunter's sixth sense; something was off. Maybe it was the fact that he had not spotted them in daylight before; maybe his refusal to leave Revelation Pass with Quimby as the killer had put a target on his back.

Across the crowd he saw Tootie in her blond wig, face strained and dark pouches nesting beneath her eyes. A spike of guilt hit him. He'd spent most of the night awake, weighing a decision that would bring them both pain, but which might be necessary to keep her from danger after this case was over. Finding his concentration wavering, he forced the thought from his mind.

Pastor Bill droned on, the townsfolk hanging on every word. Hannigan edged backward, careful not to attract attention. No one seemed to pay him any mind.

It took him a good fifteen minutes to work his way out of the gathering. Once free, he moved down the boardwalk to the front of the former marshal's office, then backed into an alley that ran beside the place. He located a rear door and breathed a relieved sigh. Prying the boards off the front door would likely have attracted the notice of one of the hardcases, raised an alarm.

This door had boards nailed above and below the handle, but they were thin, loosely nailed. He gripped the first and pulled. Nails pulled loose with a shriek, but not one loud enough to carry beyond the alley. He tossed the board to the ground and yanked the second one loose, then pitched it atop the first. He grasped the handle, finding it wouldn't turn. Jamming a shoulder hard against the door, he tried to force it open, but it was constructed of heavy wood, wouldn't budge.

He slid the Bowie knife from his boot sheath and wedged it between the frame and door just above the lock. Sweat streaked down his face by the time he'd gouged enough wood loose to make a second attempt at forcing the door. After sheathing his blade, he slammed a shoulder against the door, which shuddered, splinters tearing free around the lock. Drawing back, he snapped a kick just above the lock and the door bounded inward.

As he stepped into the building, a musty smell assailed his nostrils. The room was small, with a bank of two cells flanking the back wall. A desk and table sat towards the front. The gunrack on the south wall was empty and an over-turned coffee pot lay on the table. A blanket of dust covered everything.

Spotting no wanted dodgers lying about, he went to the desk and began pulling open drawers, hoping he'd have some luck.

He discovered a stack in the bottom drawer and set them on the desktop. After blowing a cloud of dust from the papers, he leaned over them, back to the door, studying each in turn. He had made it three-quarters down the stack when he stopped, his pulse picking up a beat.

'Christ...' he muttered, gaze locking on the gaunt face peering back at him from the dodger. William H. McKee. Wanted in four states and two territories for at least five murders, two of them nuns. Guilty of vicious attacks on women, multiple robberies. He remembered the poster now; he'd seen it just over two years back, while working on another case. After learning some of McKee's background, he'd considered chasing down the bandit. McKee and his men had roamed freely throughout Colorado, then vanished into thin air, hadn't been seen since. Rumor held they'd been ambushed by Indians.

But McKee hadn't vanished. He'd laid claim to Centerville, molded it into some schismatic heaven and hell. Bill McKee, alias Pastor Bill – likely Amy Breck's killer, way Hannigan figured it, though he still had no concrete proof or motive. The dodger gave him cause to bring the man in on past charges, if not the Breck killing; that was good enough for the moment. Given time, he reckoned he could force confessions out of Hanely and Hallet once McKee was in custody and posed no danger to them.

He gathered up the poster, rolled it into a tight tube, then jammed it in his belt.

Something moved behind him. The slightest rustle of clothing reached his ears; the tiniest scuff of a boot on wood sent a wave of chills along his spine.

Reacting on years of trail-forged instinct, he whipped around, throwing up an arm just as a knife slashed towards his back. A glimpse was enough to recognize the attacker: Jenkins, the blocky hardcase from the saloon.

The blade shredded his shirt and sliced a gash across his forearm but the wound was superficial. Momentum carried the Bowie past him. With a *thuck* the knife-tip buried itself in the top of the desk top.

The hardcase's fingers went bone-white as he fought to wrench it loose. Hannigan snapped an awkward punch that carried little power. It collided with the man's jaw just enough to get his attention but not enough to prevent him from plucking the knife free.

The manhunter stumbled backwards a step as Jenkins whisked the blade in a wide arc. The blade cleaved through fabric, drawing a pencil-thin furrow across Hannigan's belly.

A grin spread the hardcase's lips as he attempted to backhand the knife for a killing swipe. Hannigan pivoted, upper body arching ninety degrees, right leg sweeping up. His boot-heel clacked from the hardcase's knifehand. Jenkins howled and the Bowie flew from his grip.

Before Hannigan could set himself again, arms locked about him from the back, pinning his arms to his sides.

With the manhunter trapped in the grip a of second assailant, Jenkins stepped in, the grin back on his face. He sent a fist straight down the trail. Hannigan jerked his head sideways but couldn't avoid the blow entirely. Knuckles glanced from his cheek, skidded past, straight into the nose of the man holding him.

The second hardcase bellowed and wetness splattered Hannigan's cheek, blood from the man's mashed nose. The manhunter gave him no time to recover. He stamped on an instep and the hardcase released his hold as if he'd suddenly grabbed a bear in the dark. Hannigan whirled, saw the man, Jasper, the bald hardcase with a scarred neck, stagger back, clutching his bloody nose while screeching expletives.

A split second later, Hannigan pivoted, lunged at Jenkins, swinging an uppercut. His knuckles clacked from the man's jaw with the sound of a gunshot. Pain rang through the manhunter's fist. Jenkins staggered back on wobbly legs.

A fist smashed into the back of Hannigan's head. The manhunter stumbled forward, sparks exploding before his vision. Thunder pounded in the back of his skull.

More on instinct than skill, he swung around, off balance, but positioned well enough to roll Jasper off a shoulder as the hardcase charged, fist cocked for a finishing blow. Jasper crashed into Jenkins, who had recovered enough to come forward again.

Hannigan's breath beat out in searing gasps. His heart pounded. The room shimmered before his vision and he had the feeling that dynamite was going off in the back of his head.

The two hardcases panicked, apparently neither confident they could take down the manhunter on strength alone now that they had lost the advantage. Their hands went for their guns at nearly the same instant.

Neither showed speed nor skill. Their sweeps were clumsy, their hands shaking, reaction times slowed by too much thinking about the opponent before them.

Hannigan's own draw was unencumbered by intimidation or hesitation. That draw was a part of his very makeup now, lightning-quick, pinpoint accurate. His Peacemaker came up in a blur, triggering a shot that lifted Jenkins clean off his feet and hurled him backward into the small table. The table buckled, Jenkins flopping down atop it in a death dance. Blood blossomed like the crimson lily on his shirt, just above his heart.

Jasper, shocked by the sight of his partner's demise, hesitated, then fumbled with bringing his gun level.

Hannigan put a hole right between his eyes. Jasper pitched straight backward and slammed into the floor.

Hannigan's blood raced and sweat poured down his face. He stood panting in the silence that only death could bring, then holstered his gun, confident the blasts had attracted no attention. He'd made another mistake in letting those men get the jump on him again. He'd been lucky this time, but he wasn't a man who trusted luck. It was time to move on McKee and find out just what the hell was going on in this town before another mistake buried him.

The sermon finished and the crowd wandered off, placid faces alight with that lifeless smile Tootie was starting to despise. Throughout the sermon she'd seen the gaunt preacher's gaze fall on her more times than was comfortable, each look bringing a poorly hidden message of lust to his eyes. He might have managed to mesmerize the townsfolk, elicit their mechanical 'amens' and blind obedience, but his motives were plain to her. He was a Janus and had his sights set on Hannah Garret. Why? Suspicious? Or merely wantonness? Had he done the same to Amy Breck? How about

195

Quimby's daughter?

She had seen Hannigan slip away early on. She wondered if he'd had any success at the marshal's office. She hoped so; she was getting a notion that the faster they tied things up here the better. A niggling voice at the back of her mind told her her disguise as Hannah Garret was close to being compromised. The only question was how long the preacher would wait before trying something.

Intending to get back to the newspaper office, she turned, suddenly facing two men who had come up behind her. She cursed herself for being too distracted to hear their approach. Hannigan wasn't the only one who'd let emotion cloud skill, she reckoned.

'Miss Garret...' Hallet grabbed one of her arms. Hanely took the other.

'What is the meaning of this?' she said in a demanding tone, having little doubt she could put down either man if she had to, but playing up her role until she knew what they intended.

'Please, don't make trouble, Miss Garret,' Hanely said, his voice shaky. 'We have some information regarding Miss Quimby's departure.'

She gave the man a suspicious rise of her

eyebrow. 'What information? Why would it matter to me? Why can't you tell me here?'

'Just come with us, Miss Garret.' Hallet urged her forward. 'You can get back to your job at the paper after we're finished.'

He was lying. She heard it in his voice and saw it in his expression. The only thing that kept her from kicking his saddle-bags to the moon was the sometimes reckless curiosity she possessed; she couldn't claim that it was a strong point. However, she reckoned she could take care of herself if need be.

'Where are we going?' she asked, as they guided her towards the boardwalk.

'To church.' Hallet smiled. She didn't care for the smugness in it.

'Church? Why would we be going there?'

Hallet looked at her for a moment with curiosity and she wondered why.

'What happened to your accent?' the newspaperman asked and she realized she had slipped and forgotten to put it on. She cursed herself again. A stupid oversight, one she never would have made a couple months ago.

'Why, I declare, sometimes when I get all flustered it pure escapes me.' She was over-doing it but it likely didn't matter anymore.

Suspicion strengthened in Hallet's eyes,

but he kept quiet.

As they led her along the sidewalk she decided maybe it wasn't such a good idea to let them take her after all. Bill might well have more men waiting with him at the church and Hannigan was nowhere around to help her should she need it. Maybe she had grown too reliant on his backup, or maybe she had just started to doubt herself, but the odds of a lone confrontation likely weren't in her favor.

Something on her face must have given her thoughts away. Hallet's bony fist suddenly collided with her temple. It hit hard and perfect and her legs went out from beneath her. The two men heaved her up by the arms, half-carrying, half-dragging her. Through her dazed mind she heard Hanely ask Hallet just what the hell he thought he was doing hitting a woman.

'Something isn't right here, Hanely. Not right at all.' The newspaperman shook his head, face grim.

A few moments later they dragged her up the church steps and the musty odor of old books and varnish filled her nostrils. The smell revived her some, but they had her half-way down the aisle by the time her feet found the floor. The hauled her before the altar, keeping hold of her arms when they stopped.

'Ah, Brothers Hanely and Hallet, I see you have brought our guest.' He stood there like a skeletal peacock with ice in his eyes and absolutely no compassion in his manner. Beside him stood Bartlett and another man, a hardcase she didn't recognize. Bill's gaze raked her form, lingering at curves.

'What is wrong with her?' the preacher asked, noticing her dazed state.

'Hallet hit her.' Disgust laced Hanely's voice.

'I don't think she's who she says she is,' Hallet put in hastily. 'Her accent comes and goes.'

Bill's eyes narrowed. 'We'll put her downstairs with the other one for now. If she isn't Hannah Garret I'm sure by the time I'm done with her I'll know it.' He gave her a smile that said exactly what he planned to do, the same thing that fella had tried all those years ago at the home.

The notion brought an uncharacteristic burst of panic to her mind. Planting her feet and stiffening her carriage, she wrenched her arms loose, taking Hanely and Hallet by surprise. She lunged at Bill, bringing up a knee and burying it in his groin. The preacher blew out an explosive breath and doubled.

The two hardcases dove for her. She threw a kick at the first, but a bout of dizziness ruined her balance and she missed. The men grabbed her and she made them regret it. Her teeth plunged into a forearm and Bartlett let out a bleat, quickly letting go. She kicked his shin for good measure and tried to jam her fingers up the second man's nose and yank. The second hardcase jerked his head away then cracked a left hook across her jaw. Her head rocked, but she refused to go down.

Bartlett recovered enough to make a grab at her hair. The blond wig came loose in his hands and he stared at it stupidly for a moment before throwing it aside. She turned to confront him, both fists coming up in a defensive posture, but the second hard-case grabbed her from behind about the ribs and hoisted her off the floor. He squeezed until she could no longer breathe. A moment later she went limp, half-conscious, gasping.

Bill straightened, fury riding his eyes. 'Take her out to the edge of town and give her the same goddamn treatment we gave the Breck girl. This woman ain't no South-ern belle.'

'Who the hell is she?' Bartlett asked, face puzzled.

Pastor Bill dragged a forearm across his mouth, wiping spittle from his lips. 'Damned if I know but I bet she's workin' with Hannigan. Get rid of her.'

'Are you goddamn loco?' Hanely asked suddenly, shaking his head. 'Hanging that Breck girl's what got us into this mess in the first place! Now you want to do it again? You've plumb lost your mind, McKee. I won't tolerate any more of this.'

All semblance of sanity washed from the pastor's colorless eyes. He grabbed the Smith & Wesson from Bartlett's holster and triggered two shots directly into Hanely's chest. The banker coughed a spray of blood and pitched backward, hitting the floor with a thud.

Bill turned to Hallet, face crimson. 'You care to raise any doubts as to my sanity as well, Brother Hallet?'

Hallet gave a jerky shake of his head. 'No, sir. You're as sane as I am, Pastor.'

Bill remained silent for long minutes, gaze locked on Hallet, who visibly trembled. 'Go back to your newspaper. Stay there till I make sure Hannigan's dead. You'll be running the lottery from now on.'

Hallet nodded and couldn't get out of the church fast enough.

Bill glanced at Bartlett. 'Take her out the back way. Make sure that pretty little neck of hers makes a nice snap when she hangs.'

CHAPTER TEN

Deciding first to update Tootie on Pastor Bill and his plans to bring the man in, Jim Hannigan headed to the newspaper office. The game was ended, so her disguise no longer mattered. He reckoned the sooner they got Bill into custody the sooner Revelation Pass went back to being a normal town. He would have to use some caution in arresting Bill, not knowing how many hardcases mingled with the townsfolk, but he would have Tootie ride shotgun and make sure no one got the drop on them.

He entered the newspaper office to find only Bertha Hallet. The older woman poised over a table, a quill-pen in hand as she concentrated on pages filled with handwriting, a story for the next edition of the *Standard*. She looked up as he banged the door shut. A startled look crossed her face.

'What do you want?' Her voice broke.

'Where's Hannah Garret?' Apprehension coiled in the pit of his belly. Tootie should have been here. The crowd had dispersed and she wouldn't have returned to the hotel without learning what Hannigan had discovered.

Panic jumped into the woman's eyes, confirming his fear. Something had happened.

'P-please I don't know anything.' Her voice shook and she started to quake.

'I reckon you do. And I reckon that husband of yours is involved in something a hell of a lot less noble than publishing newspapers.'

'I can't ... I can't...' She shook her head, face draining white. 'He'll hit me again...'

Hannigan shook his head. 'I'll guarantee he won't, ma'am. Please, you have to tell me where she is. Don't let what happened to Amy Breck happen to anyone else.'

Her lips moved, no sound coming out at first. Then she seemed to grip her courage and her features tightened with determination. 'I ain't sure. She didn't come back after the sermon. I swear that's the truth. I'm sure she's all right–'

He took a step further into the office. 'Are

you? We can't say that about twenty other gals, can we?'

The woman staggered a step, appearing as if she might go down. She clutched the edge of the table to hold herself up. 'It wasn't his fault–'

'Why're you protecting him, Mrs Hallet? Way he hits you?'

Her gaze dropped, guilt washing over her face. 'I'm sorry, Mr Hannigan. I'm just an old woman. He's all I got.'

Hannigan didn't understand it. The woman lived in fear of the little bastard but when it came down to it, she tolerated his abuse at the cost of her self-respect and happiness. 'Where is your husband, Mrs Hallet? He with Pastor Bill again? He have something to do with Hannah not being here?'

She looked up, tears shimmering in her eyes. 'He's just scared, that's all. That's why he hits me, to keep me from being hurt. To keep this town from bein' hurt.'

'You truly believe that, ma'am, you're just foolin' yourself. I reckon a fella who cared about you wouldn't hit you at all or take up with women at the saloon.'

He saw no shock on her face, no denial. She knew he was stating the truth. Maybe she had rationalized it, convinced herself somehow that whatever was going on in this town had driven him to his deeds. But it was a lie all the same, one that had resulted in twenty-odd women vanishing or dying.

'I can't say any more, please.' The words came with a sob.

'A girl's life's at stake, ma'am. Or maybe that's happened so many times in this town it doesn't matter to you anymore.' Hannigan's hand dropped to the butt of his Peacemaker; he let himself go loose, waiting.

The woman started to collapse, barely caught herself. Tears ran down her face. 'I did not want nothin' to happen to them, I swear. I tried to stop it with Miss Garret. I tried to make her leave.'

'Shut the hell up, you stupid old cow!' snapped a voice behind Hannigan. The manhunter spun. This time he'd known someone was behind him, inching the door open. From the corner of his eye, he'd caught sight of Hallet beyond the big front window, knew the man was coming back to the office. The Peacemaker streaked upward in a blur, bore centered between the newspaperman's eyes. Hallet stopped dead, fright sweeping over his features.

'That's a goddamn nasty way to talk to your loving wife, Hallet. The old fool still cares about you, despite what you've obviously done to her and to this town.'

Hallet's eyes darted and he tried to steady himself. 'I haven't done a thing, Hannigan. Get the hell out of my office!' The bravado rang false, the man's voice shaking.

Hannigan snapped the Peacemaker sideways, clacking Hallet full across the cheek with the gate. Hallet staggered, blood dribbling from a cut on his cheek. He whimpered, staggering sideways.

The manhunter holstered his gun, then grabbed Hallet and hurled him into a table stacked with unrolled paper. The table held and Hallet rolled off, crashing to the floor, groaning.

Hannigan grabbed two handfuls of the newspaperman's shirt and hoisted him to his feet, jamming him against the wall. 'Where the goddamn hell is Tootie?'

'Tootie?' Puzzlement mixed with the pain and fear in the man's eyes.

'Hannah, Hannah Garret.'

'I don't know. I don't know.'

'That ain't the answer I was lookin' for.' Hannigan slammed him into the wall and Hallet's entire body rattled. The manhunter was prepared to beat the man to within an inch of his life if it meant finding out what happened to Tootie.

'Please, please, don't hurt me...' Hallet's voice dropped to a pathetic whine.

'That what your wife says when you beat her, Hallet? That what those twenty gals asked before they went to their deaths?'

'They ain't dead, least none of them 'cept the Breck girl.'

Hannigan pressed his face close to Hallet's. 'How the hell you know that?'

Hallet's lips trembled, blood dribbling from his mouth. 'Bill, he makes us hold a lottery and pick a gal each month. We bring her to him after. I overheard him talkin' with his man, Bartlett, one day. He finds rich Mexican men and sells them virgins.'

'And Amy Breck?'

'She...'

Hannigan banged Hallet's head against the wall, but not hard enough to knock him unconscious.

'She was soiled. We didn't know. Bill didn't want her, so he got powerful angry and hanged her.'

'That what he intends to do with Hannah Garret? Sell her to some rich fella?'

Hallet's eyes fluttered and terror glittered like chips of black ice. An explosion of dread in Hannigan's belly nearly caused him to break Hallet's scrawny neck.

'You want to live out this day you best tell me, Hallet.'

'He'll – he'll kill me. He'll kill me.'

Hannigan let go with one hand and snatched his Peacemaker from its holster again. He jammed the bore against Hallet's temple.

The newspaperman shuddered. Sweat poured down his face. Bertha Hallet gasped.

'He sent his men out with her, to the edge of town, to hang her like Amy Breck. He discovered she wasn't who she said she was.'

'Christ.' Hannigan hurled Hallet sideways. The newspaperman crashed to the floor, mewing like a kicked cat.

The manhunter was already through the door and holstering his gun by the time Hallet landed. He spotted a horse tethered to a rail and ran for it. With no time to get to the livery and saddle his own, the spindly bay would have to do. He hoisted himself into the saddle and jerked the reins, sending the mount into a gallop through the street.

John Hallet pushed himself up to hands and knees, then grabbed the edge of the table to haul himself to his feet. He gave his cowering wife a glare that said he'd take out his humiliation on her later.

The sound of the door opening made his stomach plunge with the thought that Hannigan had returned to harass him further. But, as he whirled and saw the man framed by sunlight in the doorway, he knew it would be much worse than that. Pastor Bill looked like a demonic angel come to call, his face placid yet threatening in a way Hallet couldn't have described.

'Oh, Brother Hallet, it appears you've encountered some difficulty.'

Hallet licked his lips. 'What – what are you doing here?'

'My men never returned after trailing Hannigan from the crowd. I came looking for them.' Bill stepped into the room. 'Imagine my surprise when I saw Mr Hannigan storming from your office, only to steal a horse and ride hell-bent for the edge of town. Where could he be going, Brother Hallet? Surely you would not tell him about Miss Garret...'

Hallet's face drained of all its color as Bill's pale eyes locked with his. 'It – it wasn't my fault. Hannigan, he–'

'I know, he threatened you. It couldn't be helped. Just how much did you tell him, Brother Hallet?' Bill closed the door and came a few steps closer to the newspaperman. Bertha stood rigid, gripping the table edge with bleached fingers.

Hallet had backed up a pace, fear sending a surge of nausea through his belly.

'I-I–'

'Oh, Brother Hallet, I fear you told him everything.'

'I – he was going to kill me...' Hallet suddenly felt his mouth moving but no sound coming out.

'Of course.' Bill smiled the spider smile. 'Let's speak no more of it. I understand your predicament completely.'

'You do?' Relief started to well within Hallet. It died an instant later as Bill reached into his suitcoat pocket and brought out a derringer.

'This is the gun that killed poor Mr Quimby, Brother Hallet. I took possession of it after Hannigan finished examining the body. Kind of him to leave it for me, don't you think?'

Hallet closed his eyes. A scream from his wife followed by the sound of a shot came a second later.

The world whirled before Tootie's vision. She felt herself hurled over a saddle, then the jouncing of the horse beneath her as

Bartlett and the other hardcase guided the mount through a back street towards the edge of town.

She must have blacked out for a moment because she was suddenly aware that the horse had stopped. Hands grabbed her, hauling her into a sitting position. Some of the haze cleared from her mind and the terrain stopped vibrating before her vision. She sat atop a palomino. Around her stood cottonwoods, and, beyond, in the short distance, the town of Revelation Pass. Bartlett had hold of her arm, his fingers digging in and sending spikes of pain to her fingertips. A pleased expression played over his lips. The man enjoyed murder.

The second man unlimbered a rope from his saddle then draped it over a sturdy cottonwood branch after fashioning a rough noose. Bartlett switched his grip to the reins and led her horse beneath the rope. The other man pulled a Smith & Wesson and kept it leveled on her, in case she recovered enough to put up a fight. She tried to claw at Bartlett, but was still too stunned to function properly. He jammed a fist into her belly, sending a surge of bile into her throat. The blow ended any resistance of which she was capable. She slumped in the saddle.

Bartlett returned to his horse, the other man following suit. After mounting they edged up beside her. The second hardcase reached over and straightened her torso, while Bartlett slipped the rope over her head.

It was over. She was going to die without ever having made love to Hannigan and, worse yet, never having told him she loved him. She could face death, had always known that in her line of work it was a constant companion, but never to have experienced what a normal woman had, a family, a life with someone who returned every feeling she considered worthy of feeling ... that was something she couldn't face.

'Avenge me, Hannigan...' she whispered, then: 'I love you...'

The rope jerked tight about her neck. One of the men laughed as he slapped the palomino on the flank and sent it careening out from under her. Her neck didn't snap, but a horrendous pressure cut all air off from her lungs and strands of hemp bit deep into the soft flesh of her throat. She clawed at the noose to no avail. Sparkles of light exploded before her vision. From the distance the pounding of hoofbeats rose to a thunderous roar but all she could hear was the throbbing laugh of all she'd never been...

Jim Hannigan had never considered himself a religious man but he whispered a prayer now that he would reach Tootie before they killed her. He could already see two hardcases up ahead, placing a noose around her neck. His hands bleached as he gripped the reins tighter, heels pounding the horse's sides to spur it beyond its limits.

He had to reach her in time. He couldn't lose her, couldn't let her be taken from him after the way they had left each other last night, couldn't let her die without knowing how he felt.

Closer.

Sweat poured down his face and chest, ran in streams beneath his arms. His heart pounded; his blood roared in his ears.

'Noooo!' he yelled, anguish flooding his voice, as a hardcase slapped the horse beneath Tootie, leaving her dangling in space.

It gave him only a small measure of relief that she pried at the noose. At least the jolt hadn't snapped her neck. That meant he still had precious instants before she strangled. 'Hold on, goddammit!' he uttered, every nerve driving him forward.

One hand came loose from the reins and

213

swept towards the Peacemaker at his hip. The other slowed the bay while he brought up the gun, a move that took every ounce of willpower and skill in him. He was no horseman. He nearly lost his balance and ended up thrown. Only sheer determination to reach Tootie held him in the saddle.

He blasted a shot that missed and the men's horses started to dance about at the sound of gunfire. One of the men already had a gun out; he managed a return shot. The bullet missed by feet as Hannigan angled his mount left.

Pulling hard on the reins, the manhunter brought the bay to a skidding stop. The other two still hadn't gained complete control of their mounts.

Hannigan triggered a shot. The man with the gun flew backwards out of the saddle and landed flat on the hardpack, unmoving. Crimson swelled on his chest.

Bartlett made an attempt to get at his gun while trying to calm his horse, but never reached it. Hannigan swung his aim and blasted him out of the saddle.

Wasting no time surveying the dead men, the manhunter leaped from the saddle, feet hitting dirt in a run. Dropping his Peacemaker, he wrapped both arms around

Tootie's legs, lifting. Releasing one hand, he lifted his leg and snatched the knife from its boot sheath. He could barely reach the rope at the back of her head, but strands snapped as the blade tip sawed through. Lowering her to the ground, he tossed the knife into the dirt and pried at the noose. He loosened it and yanked it over her head. She coughed with violent shudders, tears streaming from her eyes. She clung to him, and he held her, shaking with relief.

'J-Jim ... I...' she tried to speak but her words came raspy, made her cough harder.

'Shhh, don't try to talk yet. You'll be OK. You'll be OK.' He swallowed at the emotion choking his throat.

The sound of hoofs brought him from his thoughts and his head lifted. A man slowed to a stop on a roan, the expression on his gaunt face barely human. Vicious promise raged in Pastor Bill's colorless eyes like wildfire. He held a derringer in his hand, leveled on Hannigan.

'You've ruined everything, Mr Hannigan. Everything. You should never have defiled the Lord's town. His vengeance will be swift and final.' His tone had lost some of his usual tranquillity. Hannigan saw a man barely able to rein in his rage, a man struggling with something dark embedded into his very make-up.

Hannigan's eyes narrowed. 'You're no man of the Lord, McKee. You're a murderer and a thief, pure and simple.'

Bill's face pinched. 'Ah, so you know.' He eased from the saddle. While keeping the derringer pointed at Hannigan, who gently lowered Tootie's upper body to the ground, he went to Bartlett's corpse, exchanging his derringer for a Smith & Wesson.

Hannigan's gun lay a few feet away, to his left. He saw no chance to reach it. He came up onto one knee, one hand on the ground, fingers splayed.

'Got the idea to become a reverend from a pulp book, Mr Hannigan. Seemed fitting. 'Cept one thing about those books always bothered me. The way the villain always talked too damn much at the end and got himself killed. So if you'll forgive me forgoing a parting prayer...'

Bill's finger twitched on the trigger.

Hannigan, who'd kept his eyes locked with Bill's, saw the fraction of thought that came before action. He rolled, timing the move perfectly, as the preacher pulled the trigger. The roll, over a shoulder, brought him over his Bowie knife and he clasped it as he came up into a squat.

Bill's lead drilled into the ground where Hannigan had knelt an instant before. The manhunter surged to his feet, flinging the Bowie. The knife flew from his grip, propelled with all the force he could muster.

Bill let out a startled gasp, suddenly looked down at the hilt of the blade sticking out of his chest. The Smith & Wesson dropped from his grip. He collapsed, blood gushering from around the blade.

'Praise the Lord...' whispered Hannigan.

'I can't thank you enough for rescuing me from that room, Mr Hannigan,' said Alyssa Quimby. 'I was frightened out of my wits. They told me they were going to send me to Mexico with some men.'

Hannigan nodded, mood somber as he stood outside the hotel, saddle-bags slung over a shoulder. The brassy sun glared from the early-morning sky, promising another scorcher of a day. Folks wandered the streets as before, but a sort of aimlessness burdened their gait now and the smiles on their faces had vanished.

He'd discovered Alyssa Quimby locked in a room beneath the church after searching the place for any of Bill's remaining men.

Any leftover hardcases had faded into the woodwork or left town after Hannigan rode in with Bill McKee's body slung over a saddle. He'd also found Hanely's body lying in the aisle. Bertha Hallet had informed him her husband was dead. She'd closed the newspaper down and gone into seclusion.

'Wish I could have done the same for the Breck girl and the rest, but I reckon there's little chance of finding them now.'

She looked at the ground, deep sadness on her face. Her father had given her up to Bill, then paid the price. He couldn't imagine how that must feel. She was a strong girl, handling it as well as could be expected, but something in her eyes no longer held the naivety of youth.

'I'm a reporter. Least I thought of myself that way. My father shielded me from the lottery, though I saw the things that went on here at night and saw the strange looks on the folks' faces. I was afraid to question it. Maybe if I had ... well, maybe things wouldn't have turned out the way they did and those girls wouldn't have gone missing. I have some relatives two towns over. I'll go there and see if I can't get a newspaper to take me on. With help maybe I can find some of the girls. Maybe there's a chance...'

He doubted it, but wouldn't dash her hope. She needed something to hang onto after what she'd gone through. 'There's a fella named Breck.' He reached into his pocket and pulled out a slip of paper with an address, handing it to her. 'He lost a daughter. Might help him come to terms if you told him what you went through. Might help you, too.'

She nodded, lips grim. 'I'll do that, Mr Hannigan.' She looked about at the folks milling along the boardwalk. 'What do you reckon will become of this place?'

He shrugged. 'They been this way for a spell. Reckon they'll feel a loss, then things will slowly go back to normal. I'll telegraph the territorial marshal. He'll send someone down to help things along and see to it that Bill's gang don't resurface. Rest is up to them.'

'Rest is in the hands of God, Mr Hannigan.' She gave him a warm smile.

He forced one back, not entirely convinced, and tipped a finger his hat. He left her standing on the boardwalk.

As he reached the livery a heaviness settled over his soul. He couldn't force the image of Tootie hanging out of his mind. In fact, it had kept him awake all night, put the final word on the course he'd been mulling over for the past few weeks. This was for the best, he told himself, leaving her in her room while he rode off, though it felt damned awful. He cared about her too much to risk her life any further. In the process he would sacrifice his existence to days spent alone, forever empty, but it had to be.

'You didn't really think you could ride off without me, did you?'

He stopped just inside the double livery doors, the musky aroma of hay and dung in his nostrils and the sensation of lead plunging into his belly. She stood next to a stall, wearing a riding-skirt and powder-blue blouse, her horse already saddled. A hurt expression rode her features.

Guilt washed over him and he had a hard time looking her in the eye. 'It's best that way, Tootie. I can't be worried over you getting killed anymore.'

She cocked an eyebrow. 'That what you're truly worried about?'

The question unsettled him and she had that look again, the one that bored deep into his being and laid his secrets bare.

'I won't risk your life anymore,' he restated stubbornly, feeling the guilt deepen.

'It's my risk to take. I took it before you

came along, so don't give me excuses. You're just lying to me and to yourself if you think that's all there is to it.'

'We both made mistakes on this case, any one of them enough to get us dead right quick in this business.'

She pushed away from the stall door and came closer to him, arms folded. Her mahogany eyes narrowed, prying at his soul. 'You want to ride out of here alone, you go right ahead. But first you tell me honestly you don't give a damn about me and don't want me anymore.'

He looked away, unable to hold her gaze. He couldn't tell her that. He could lie to himself about his reasons for running, but he couldn't say he didn't care. Suddenly he wondered if he could have even gone through with leaving her behind. A nagging voice in the back of his mind told him he would have made it no more than a mile or two before turning back.

His voice came low and he couldn't drag an explanation out of his heart. 'Reckon I best saddle up. We got a ride ahead of us.'

She smiled, but it was more fragile than usual. 'I knew you couldn't live without me.' Her tone didn't quite carry the confidence it should have. The hurt of finding that he would even consider leaving her behind was still too fresh, the wound open. It would take time to regain a piece of her trust, which he had betrayed. He reckoned he was the world's biggest sonofabitch.

Turning his head away, his voice lowered, a peace offering. 'It scared the hell out of me thinking I wouldn't reach you in time. When I saw you hanging there…'

'Shhh…' She turned his face towards her and placed a finger to his lips, then drew it away. 'You had my back. That's all I can ask … for now.'

He nodded, wishing he could give her more, but he couldn't.

He'd nearly worked up a simple 'I'm sorry' when she hauled off and slapped him. The slap stung like hell and annoyed him more than a little. 'What the hell was that for?'

She grinned and went to her horse, grabbing the reins, then looking back to him. '*That* was for being a bastard…'

She didn't stop giving him an earful for the first five miles of their journey.

The publishers hope that this book has given you enjoyable reading. Large Print Books are especially designed to be as easy to see and hold as possible. If you wish a complete list of our books please ask at your local library or write directly to:

Dales Large Print Books
Magna House, Long Preston,
Skipton, North Yorkshire.
BD23 4ND